# KEEPING KYLE

## A HOCKEY ALLIES BACHELOR BID MM ROMANCE

## JEFF ADAMS

BIG GAY
Media

# Keeping
# KYLE

# JEFF ADAMS

## HOCKEY ALLIES BACHELOR BID MM ROMANCES

**Hot hockey players on the auction block...**
Win a date with a professional hockey player during All Star weekend in Chicago. From leading scorers to fan favorites to guys you love to hate, watch the players strut their stuff in support of the Hockey Allies charity. Place a bid. You just might find someone to keep you warm.
**One night. One bid. One hockey bachelor auction... could change everything.**

*Guarding Garrett* – RJ Scott
*Loving Layne* – VL Locey
*Keeping Kyle* – Jeff Adams
*Scoring Slater* – Susan Scott Shelley
*Absolving Ash* – Chantal Mer

# ONE

## KYLE

"You ready for the auction?" In the locker room, my younger brother Bobby started stripping out of his gear as I did the same. The other guys from our pickup game changed around us. "Got a fancy suit so you look extra hot for the bidders?"

"Did you just say hot?" I shot a scowl at Bobby.

"What? I want my brother to get high bids. Family honor on the line and all."

This locker room always took me back about a dozen years to a time when being jammed in together with a bunch of friends to change was a common occurrence. Bobby played on a recreational team in Chicago, and when I was in town, he always organized a pickup game with some of his friends and teammates.

This weekend, I wasn't here with the rest of the Detroit Arsenal though. The NHL All-Star Game would be played here, and not only had I—Arsenal center Kyle Pressgrove— been selected to play for the Western Conference, but I'd also be competing in the skills competition for the title of fastest skater.

1

An unofficial event for the weekend that I'd gotten involved in was the Hockey Allies hockey bachelor auction to raise money for its work to ensure equality in hockey regardless of a player's orientation or gender identity. I'm always ready to help a good cause, but being paraded out for bids scared me a bit—actually more than a bit. I'm trying not to focus on that.

Bobby wasn't helping.

"Hey, Bobby, is it okay if I bid on him?" My face heated, and I suddenly felt self-conscious in just my jock shorts as one of Bobby's friends added to my embarrassment.

"Of course, as long as you treat him to a great date if you win."

"Please stop." I buried my face in my hands, hoping to will the redness away before looking back to Bobby. It wasn't easy though. Many of his friends chuckled. I couldn't blame them for that since I would've laughed too in their shoes. "As my brother, you are not allowed to talk to me about being hot... or not being hot... or whatever. Jesus. I can't believe I let you and Garrett"—or G, as Bobby and I called him—"talk me into this thing. And I've got to be up there against Mister ESPN. Really? I get that it's a good cause, but what if I'm won by some creepy stalker type?" A valid concern since Garrett's been dealing with that stuff. "And what if no one bids at all?"

"Have you seen you?"

Why? Why did he keep going?

"The hockey body. The five o'clock shadow. Those piercing eyes. I know what people say about you online. In fact, you could give people what they want and show more skin, maybe an open shirt. As for G, it's ESPN's loss they didn't pick you."

I snorted out a laugh. Garrett Howell, a center for the

Burlington Dragons, had a perfect ESPN body, and he deserved that cover, even though I'd given him a fair amount of shit for it. My brother and I had been friends with him since we all played juniors. He even stayed with us and essentially become our third brother.

We'd also all come out to each other.

He'd been the third person I'd told, after Mom and Bobby. He told me shortly after he moved in with us because he'd wanted me to know, so I told him too. We'd been a great support system for each other over the years, and Mom and Bobby always had his back too. All his social media activity and the cover had brought some unwanted attention though. Even though he had someone watching out for him, I still worried.

"You got the family looks too, you know." I looked to divert the discussion. "You conveniently forget that sometimes."

"But they work better on your athletic build."

We weren't twins, but Dad had apparently had dominant genes, and we carried a lot of his features—the light blue eyes, the nose that was a little too small for our heads, jet black hair, and the near constant scruff. We had his height too at just over six feet, though I had a couple inches on Bobby.

He was also a bean pole. Where I'd filled out in high school, Bobby remained on the thin side. He'd tried to change that, but no amount of weight training did much to bulk him up.

Luckily, we got along great. Sure, we did some picking on each other, but there was no doubt—ever—that we were tight. I think it helped that we were only a year apart, but our parents also made sure we treated each other right. They didn't put up with any petty sibling rivalry.

But Mom wouldn't have even chastised him about what he was doing to me now. Odds were, she'd have joined in.

"If you were part of the lineup, I'd bid on you, Bobby, but I don't want Seb coming after me," another of Bobby's friends chimed in.

I grabbed my phone from the shelf in the locker I used and snapped Bobby's slightly reddened face. I rarely embarrassed him, no matter how hard I tried. Even in middle and high school, he had a high immunity for it. Somehow his friend pushed the right button, and now I had some proof. I took a couple more pics as the redness darkened.

"No fair, bro." He tried for the phone, but I snatched it out of reach.

"Totally fair. Seb's going to love them." Bobby's fiancé couldn't get much of a rise out of him either—which we both attributed to his even-keeled therapist persona.

Bobby looked at his phone, which chirped with Mom's tone. "She's boarded and seems on time. She used way too many emojis to end her message."

I looked over his shoulder. "Is that every excited one there is? Wow."

Mom's enthusiasm was bubbling over for this weekend. She might have been even more excited than me when the news broke that I'd been selected for this year's game. It was my first time and, of course, a huge honor. My game isn't flashy, and I'm not a face of the team or anything, but I go out and get my job done and have acquired some fans along the way. To be recognized after seven years had me pretty damn giddy.

"You expected anything less?" Bobby asked as we headed for the showers. "I know how proud I am of you, and she's got to be like a million times more so."

She'd been one of my major champions since I first

4

laced up skates. A lot of great things were on tap for this weekend, but having my family on hand was the best part. She'd wanted to come to the auction, but we'd convinced her that wasn't a good idea. As much as Bobby liked to harass and embarrass me, Mom coming to the auction was too much since we had no idea how the crowd would behave. Turned out, G had also hoped she wouldn't be there since he thought of her as a mom too.

"You know, it wouldn't hurt if the high bidder takes you on a nice date. It's been too long for you."

"Not this again." The words came out wrapped in a groan. Bobby liked to discuss my lack of a relationship—he'd always dated more than me—but he'd escalated once he and Sebastian settled down.

"Don't give me that. If you gave yourself half a chance, you could find the right guy. You're not even trying."

"You know how my..."

"Schedule is. Yeah, yeah, yeah. And I know how chill the off-season is, where you could start something that lasts." Bobby shifted from a mocking tone to something I imagined he used on his patients. "You're going to need a date to my wedding, after all, come July. As wildly important as family is to you, you actually should find a guy to start one with. Sebastian and I are looking forward to having kids, and I have no doubt you'd be an amazing dad too."

"Oh my God. Did Mom put you up to this because you sound just like her right now." This was an old conversation. I did want a family—but I also had people to take care of. I had to make sure Mom was okay and that Bobby had help when he needed it. Although, that was far less often over the past three years since he'd met Sebastian. Besides finding a good guy wasn't easy. The last one I thought might be dateable turned out to be a jerk, breaking up with a text.

5

"Maybe I just want to be an uncle and have built-in playdates with our kids."

"That won't be so easy if I end up across the country." Might as well deflect one uncomfortable conversation with another. I stepped to the side of a showerhead and started the water flow.

"I was going to ask about that." Bobby did the same at the shower next to mine. "Anything more concrete?"

"No." I sighed. "Wait and see at this point. The team is definitely looking to shore up defense. My agent told me just before I came down here that I fit the ideal profile for this trade. A couple others on the team do too, but I tick all the boxes. Knowing that only makes it worse. I appreciated Candace bracing me for that, but still..."

"Sorry, man. Maybe if you win the skills competition or stand out, here they won't let you go."

"Or, I make myself even more attractive to the other team."

The last thing I wanted was to leave Detroit. Unfortunately, unlike Bobby who moved away by choice, this decision was out of my hands. Thinking about it too much made me nauseous from nerves. Not only did I love my hometown, but that's where I needed to be for my family.

# TWO

## AUSTIN

"Do you think they'd be open to seeing all three concepts?" Marilyn, one of the lead designers, asked hopefully. "We can present all the usability data and elaborate on our points of view."

I adjusted my glasses, pushing them up the bridge of my nose. "I don't know the team well enough yet to know if they'd appreciate three options or if they expect a single one."

Across the table, concepts were emblazoned with the logo I'd come up with four years ago—a stylized, burnt orange, smooth font "AMDD" with "Austin Murray Digital Designs" in a crisp, easy-to-read typeface. I should know what to present to this potential client, but the importance of the presentation was causing me to second guess myself. Despite the success we'd had over the past three years, to continue to grow the company and become more profitable, we needed a lot more new business. A multi-year, multi-million-dollar contract rode on the outcome of next week's meeting to show off this work.

The board didn't like the projections for the next fiscal year if we didn't land this opportunity.

The rectangular table in the corner of my office was covered in mockups for a proposed interface for a new luxury SUV line. We'd worked to get in with this manufacturer for two years to prove we had better concepts than their current design team.

While we'd prepped for this over the past six weeks, now that we neared the end of the line, tendrils of anxiety were extending their reach into me each day. I made it worse by keeping up a façade for my team. They knew I obsessed on details—to the degree of firing off multiple emails overnight with ideas to consider—but they didn't need to see stress or doubt.

If we impressed, this enhanced interface—that used voice and touch and could be used in the car or via an app— would make its debut in this new model. Not only would it be used in the dashboard but in screens for the passengers in the back as well.

The presentation would be done on Tuesday, yet six days out, the team continued debating what to put forth. It wasn't even as minor as colors, some of it was the core of how it looked and functioned. I didn't want to make an arbitrary choice. The designers had good instincts and knew how to back up their opinions with data. In this case, three of the interfaces tested pretty equally—a credit to the team but also an impediment to making a choice.

A knock on the open door made me jump. Edginess gnawed at me, making me overreact.

Tamara—best friend, co-founder, and chief operating officer—to the rescue.

Hopefully.

"This isn't good." She dropped into a seat between me

and Marilyn. Her gaze darted between us, what was on the table, and the two other designers across from us before her focus settled on me. "I don't think you've moved since I was here two hours ago except to maybe shuffle papers on the table and put different things on the screen. Still can't decide?"

The designers shook their heads, and I shrugged.

Tamara and I met during my sophomore year at the University of Michigan. She'd been a senior and attended a showcase of technology. In only five minutes of talking, we'd discovered a mutual passion for the opportunities of good designs meshed with good tech. Once I'd graduated and she'd finished her MBA, we'd hatched AMDD to revolutionize the driver and passenger interfaces in cars.

"Clearly, the team is too good at their job." I smiled at the group. Indecisiveness didn't sit well with me, and the left side of my brain kicked the right for not putting an end to this.

"How about I take over this discussion, and we'll get you a final decision?" Tamara's expression told me I needed to say yes, but I raised an eyebrow at her instead. "You need to get out of here. Your driver's been calling because he's worried about the traffic to get you to the airport."

I picked up the tablet that displayed my top choice. "It'll be fine."

Tamara took the tablet from my hands, like I was a child she was scolding. Only she could get away with that. "You've been looking forward to this for months. We can chat from the plane, but you need to go."

She had the stern face perfected—part of what made us a great team. She knew that look would rein in my controlling nature.

"You're right." I sighed. I didn't feel like I should leave

though. I wanted to go to the All-Star Game, and the bachelor auction that was an unofficial part of the weekend's activities, but this meeting... Too much depended on it.

"Let me talk with the team." Tamara continued to make her point. "Maybe all this needs is a fresh perspective. I'm not as immersed in all of this as you all are."

I held up my hands and smiled. "All right. It's all yours. I'll check in once we're in flight."

I went to my desk and shoved a tablet and laptop in my backpack. I refrained from saying anything as the team walked Tamara through what we'd discussed.

The All-Star Game trip had been on my calendar since it was announced it would be in Chicago. I couldn't miss it being so close. Hockey had been my obsession since I was a kid. For the past few years, I've had season tickets for Arsenal games, and I convinced the board to sponsor the team too.

They didn't quite understand why I insisted on the expense, but I'd been a fan for as long as I could remember. Having AMDD associated with the team filled me with pride in the same way a job well done did.

The All-Star Game also got a lot more interesting once Kyle Pressgrove—my vote for sexiest guy in the NHL—had been selected for the game and to compete in the skills competition. I'd followed Kyle since we were freshmen in high school and he played for the Warriors. That he'd ended up with the Arsenal seemed like a dream come true because I got to watch him play live so many times during the season. I hated that trade rumors swirled around about him.

The first time I saw Kyle on the ice was burned into my brain. Long, dark hair sticking out from under his helmet got me first, and then he took the helmet off after winning. The beaming smile had my heart skipping a beat or two.

Even from a distance, he radiated happiness. I started paying attention to him at school too—subtly, since I was a geeky, gangly kid, and he was very much a star jock. His popular star status didn't keep him from being nice to everybody though, and I liked that. I never had the nerve to even say hello to him, and in a school our size, anonymity was easy.

My parents never understood my fascination with the game. They always took me to task for going to games. As a teenager, it was because I should have been studying or working. Now, they considered it a waste of hard-earned money.

The fact that Kyle, still a ridiculously handsome hockey player, was part of a bachelor auction benefitting Hockey Allies made this weekend even more special. My logical side, represented by my Dad's voice, repeated often that it was ridiculous to bid on Kyle.

I ignored that—at least as best as I could.

Why not spend time with my favorite player—and my long-time crush—and go to dinner? I'd never work up the nerve to approach him in Detroit. Sure, I could play the sponsor card to get time with him, but a charity auction was a much better excuse.

I had no idea what to expect at the auction other than they'd assembled quite a group of players to participate. The minimum bid on any of the athletes was a hundred dollars—low enough for most people to be able to afford to bid on their favorite. I would pay whatever it would take for the date with Kyle—that might be stalkerish, but I didn't care.

The money went to a great cause, so I didn't care about the cash. Admittedly, part of me just wanted to throw enough money down at the outset to win, but I didn't want to make that much of a scene. I'd just gently keep nudging the bid up until I won.

"Okay, guys, I'm gone. I'll ping you on chat as soon as I can."

"How about you open chat and wait for us to ping you?" Tamera asked as I crossed the office to where my luggage sat by the door.

Tamara tried to make sure I occasionally left the office. She was a good balance for me, often reminding me that I insisted on a work/life balance for the staff and that I deserved that too.

The weekend was going to be awesome. I'd finally meet my favorite player and catch some good hockey. Mixed in with that, we'd finish sorting out the presentation.

As soon as I got in the car, I brought up the designs on my tablet. Just because I wasn't going to talk to them for about an hour, didn't mean I couldn't pore over them and figure out the one to move forward with.

# THREE

## KYLE

IT HAD ONLY TAKEN G asking me to do the auction to say yes. We were always there for each other. Walking into the Windward Way Hotel ballroom, I hadn't expected it to be so large or for the stage to be quite as imposing.

It had a freakin' runway.

I took a deep breath to center myself. I could do this. I probably wouldn't like it, but I'd get through it. Hockey Allies was a great organization. G wouldn't get me into anything too ridiculous.

A group of players hung out to the side of the stage, and it only took me a moment to spot the instigator of this gig.

"G!" I called out as I approached.

"K!" Breaking away from the group of players, he came over. We did a quick fist bump and a longer hug. We hadn't seen each other since G had played against us at home a few weeks back. While we texted and FaceTimed a lot, nothing beat actually seeing him. "So good to see you."

"Good to see you, man. Looks like your friend put together quite the event."

"And you haven't seen half of it. They just got some of

the rough stuff done so we could rehearse. The room will be fully transformed by tomorrow night. How've you been?"

"Good, man. Really working to make myself valuable to avoid the trade. I mean, I get that it will be whatever the team decides is best, but..."

"I know." G clapped me on the back and guided me over to the rest of the guys. "You want to be one of those players who spends his career rooted in one spot. Seems harder to do these days with all concern about salary caps and random, wild trades and expansions. You never know what's going to happen."

"Are you trying to make me feel better?" I jabbed at G's ribs with my elbow, knowing exactly where his ticklish spot was.

"Hey..." He flinched and backed away. We traded smirks. "Sorry. Couldn't help but get in a dose of realism. Not to mention, Mamma P wants you to know that it's okay if you move."

I groaned. "She's talking to you about it?" She already had Bobby working on me.

"You know it." He smiled and spoke softly. "She wants you happy and not worried about her." Joining the group, he dropped that conversation. "Guys, you all know Kyle Pressgrove with Detroit."

Fist bumps and hellos went all around. I knew them, of course, but none as well as I knew G.

And, wow. Layne Coleman was here.

My inner fanboy went into overtime and tamped down the urge to tell him what an inspiration he'd been. His smooth game play and sportsmanship inspired me, not to mention the fact that he still played.

"Okay, I think everybody's here." A guy's voice boomed

over the PA, and we all gathered around the extended catwalk to listen.

The details flew fast and furious. The auction would take place after the skills competition, and we had some time to get back and prepare before the event kicked off. After the final bid, the event would continue, allowing everyone to mingle and have time with the person who had won the bidding to arrange the dates.

That was the simple part.

How to not be awkward on the catwalk was another matter. How should I do it? A normal walk? Some semblance of sexy? Any attempt at that would end up looking ridiculous. Some sort of a dance to whatever the music was? A couple guys tried that, and it looked less than good. I enjoyed dancing, but there was a big difference between doing it in a club with friends and on a stage in front of a bunch of strangers.

I'd have to talk to Bobby about how he thought I should walk. He'd never let me look like an idiot. For rehearsal, I kept it simple. I had a few hours to figure out what to do to try and *sell* myself. The guy on the PA actually said that's how we should consider it. The bidding would go on for as long as there were bids, and the MC wouldn't drag it out very long if the bidding made it over a thousand dollars.

What if I couldn't go for that much money? It'd be embarrassing to be the guy with the lowest bids or something where the auctioneer had to coax the amount up. I sent up a quick prayer that it wouldn't happen. My self-confidence usually kept me grounded, but it would already be tested here—no need to stretch the boundaries any farther.

Rehearsal zipped by. Hopefully, the event would be the same. I still needed to try on my suit for the stylist, so I dropped into a chair at one of the tables and pulled out my phone to catch up on the text messages Bobby had been sending.

"Hey, Kyle, this looks like it's gonna be quite something." David Moore, one of the PR guys from the team, sat across from me. "I snapped a couple of pics, and I'll toss them up on social media to show people how you're representing for a good cause during the weekend."

"You didn't get anything too ridiculous, did you?" I ran my hand nervously through my hair. The glint in David's eye temporarily gave me pause.

"Just you striking that pose, hand in pocket, at the end." I suppressed a groan. That pose had felt ridiculous—I'd regretted it as soon as I did it—and now it'd live forever on Instagram. "Got a couple of you with some of the other players too. We'll save the really juicy stuff for live auction posts."

Did I know about that? Sometimes I didn't pay as much attention to David as I probably should. "Serious?"

"Yeah, I'll be here. I'll post some pics. Maybe some live video. Depends on how the Wi-Fi is here. Want to make sure you get your fair share of the other media coverage too."

*Other media coverage.* Great. Now I'd have to be even more careful to not be a spaz on stage.

"Oh, I didn't know he'd be here." David looked at a guy standing in the doorway of the ballroom.

"Should I know him?"

"Maybe. He's Austin Murray. He owns AMDD. You've probably seen the logo on the scoreboard and some other signage."

Indeed I had. I liked the futuristic logo. Austin didn't look like any sponsor I'd ever met—who were usually older and in some sort of business casual attire. He wore simple jeans and a sweater along with super cute glasses perched on his nose that he'd already pushed up twice in the few seconds I'd focused on him.

"We should go say hi." David put his hand on my forearm to get me to follow him. "Dammit. He wasn't on the list of sponsors for the weekend."

Austin looked like a regular guy next door, and I kind of wanted to snuggle up to him because he looked cozy and adorable in the sweater.

Damn, thoughts like that didn't crop up often. Of course I liked looking at guys, but curling up with one didn't enter into the equation. Snuggling led to relationships, and that didn't fit in right now.

The closer we got, the more his stunning eyes stood out. I couldn't quite decide the color with the all the lights swirling around, but they were light, and they enhanced the appeal of his dark, curly hair and bit of stubble on his cheeks.

"Mr. Murray, not sure if you remember me, I'm David Moore with the Detroit PR office. It's good to see you. Are you here for the game? No one told me you were coming."

Austin looked decidedly uncomfortable, and for a moment, he tensed like he might bolt. Composure quickly replaced that though as he relaxed and pasted on a confident smile—one that I recognized from having met sponsors before who always wanted to impress. His eyes even seemed to darken a bit, like he'd flipped a switch to activate business Austin.

"Yes, of course, David. Hello. Please call me Austin. I'm just taking in the game as a fan and wanted to check out the auction—decided to leave the business behind for the weekend."

"Great. If we can do anything for you though, please just let us know. Happy to help out even while you're here as a fan. Do you know Kyle Pressgrove?"

I extended my hand, and Austin looked between me and it. Did I scare him?

"Um. Yes. Hi." He finally took my hand and cleared his throat before he spoke again. There was some of that Austin that had been on display when David first talked to him. "I'm a big fan. Great to meet you."

Despite the nervousness, his shake was strong.

"Good to meet you as well. Enjoying the city so far?"

"Just arrived a few minutes ago and noticed all this when I was checking in. It's really great that you're all taking the time to support something like this."

"I'm always happy to help organizations like Hockey Allies. My best friend helped organize it, and my brother would be disappointed if I didn't do this in his city."

"Hockey runs in the family then?"

"I think my brother would debate that." A chuckle escaped. "He feels like I got more than my fair share of the skills. He plays better than he gives himself credit for. He's a defenseman on one of the teams in the Chicago Gay Hockey Association."

"Kyle?" My name came over the PA. "Can we please get you for your final fitting?"

"I'm sorry, I've got to..."

"No worries. Um, do you think..." Austin paused to adjust his glasses, the movement making my breath catch. "Can I maybe buy my favorite player a drink after you're done?"

As I considered, David's eyes bored into me, willing me to say yes. "Sure. I can meet you in the bar in a few minutes."

The stammers he made when he got nervous only added to the cuteness that had me wanting to snuggle.

The fitting proved worse than the rehearsal. I hated fussing over my appearance, and the tugs, tweaks, hemming, and whatnot got old fast. It turned out well though—black suit, purple vest, black shirt, and matte silver tie worked well. No matter what else happened, I wouldn't be embarrassed by my appearance.

"Damn," G said as he walked out of the dressing room, handing off his clothes to one of the stylists. "Can I bid on you?"

"You can't afford me." My reply was ridiculous, but I tried to sell it with all the smugness I could muster.

He stepped up and inspected me closer. "You really do look great."

"Thanks, man. You got all the brunch details?"

"Yup. Bobby sent them. Can't wait to see Mamma P. Catch you in the morning."

We said our goodbyes just in time for another stylist to come talk about my hair. I kept it long enough that it could dry and fall pretty well on its own. For events, I usually slicked it back so it'd look more formal, and we agreed that'd work for tomorrow.

Once I changed back into my street clothes, I went to find Austin. He sat at the corner of the bar, facing the door, making him easy to spot. He studied his phone and had earbuds in. He still waved me over but held up a finger, pointed to the phone, and then held up the finger again.

The focused look as he studied his phone and talked quietly kept my attention. I'd seen three sides of Austin so far, and each sparked my interest. David would kick my ass if I hooked up with a sponsor. Hookups weren't even my thing, but I kind of wanted to be around this guy.

I ordered a ginger ale and waited. I had nothing else on deck for this evening, and tomorrow was an early brunch, a couple of fan zone activities, and then the skills competition followed by the auction.

Austin's talk centered around designs of some kind, especially colors and touch areas. Despite talking softly, I picked up a few words depending on his inflection. His expression was super serious as he swiped left and right on his phone.

From the way he talked, it didn't seem like he planned to get off the phone anytime soon. There were no telltale attempts at trying to wrap things up in terms of how he talked or with glances at me. Rather than pulling out my phone to pass the time, I watched SportsCenter on the TV behind the bar.

"I am so sorry," Austin finally said twenty minutes later. He took the earbuds out, flipped the phone over, and laid the buds on top. "How did the fitting go?"

"I'm not used to being so fawned over. I've dressed myself just fine for some twenty years now, and to have three people circling me is bonkers."

Austin held up his glass, and the bartender poured bourbon. "I hate suits, and I know you guys have to do that every game. It'd make me crazy."

"You get used to it. Even my youth coach thought it was important—showing respect for the game and our opponents. So I make sure I've got enough dress clothes to get through any road trip." I leaned closer, and Austin tilted an ear in my direction so I could share a secret. "It doesn't mean I like it though. Give me comfortable jeans and a T-shirt any day."

Austin looked intensely at me. His light brown eyes, that I now had a good look at, were gorgeous. He raised his glass. "To casual clothes." I clinked mine against it, and we took a drink. "So what does All-Star week mean for you? I was thrilled you finally got picked."

"Thanks, man. I don't think the full impact of it has hit yet. Having my mom, brother, and his fiancé in the stands tomorrow as I skate in the skills competition is... I don't know what. Not to mention..."

The phone vibrated against the bar top, and he acted like he'd ignore it, but he ultimately flipped it over. He sighed as he looked between the phone and me. "I should take this. Sorry."

I nodded. "I should go. I'm meeting up with my fam early. Are you coming to the auction?"

Austin answered the call and said, "Hold on one second." He tapped the screen, presumably to mute, and fixed me with a disappointed look that crinkled up his face. "For sure, and I'll be around the events tomorrow too."

"Cool. We'll run into each other then."

"Look forward to it." A shy smile crossed his lips for a fleeting moment before he tapped the phone screen again. He popped in his ear buds and started talking.

I downed the rest of my ginger ale, left money on the bar, and waved to Austin. He didn't acknowledge it because his screen had his full attention. Thank God my job didn't have me tied to a phone. Dragging my work around every-where would make me insane, especially if I had to pick hanging with friends and family over a phone call.

# FOUR

## AUSTIN

Kyle Pressgrove stuck in my head—that quirky smile, the broad shoulders, and the fine hairs that dusted the back of his hand and trailed up to his wrist where they disappeared under the sleeve of the Henley he wore.

But we couldn't even share a full drink without my damn phone interrupting. My reflexes kicked in, and I answered.

Our brief conversation went well, despite my heart thumping away double time because this sexy superstar—my crush for years—sat next to me.

I'd had the chance to make more of a connection before the auction—and I blew it.

Dammit.

The team had needed my attention, and I didn't have the will power to delay them for even a half hour. They continued to work, and I had to be available. I wouldn't allow anyone to be stuck waiting for something from me.

Hockey was one of the few things I gave myself—an almost sacred thing. Watching a game, everything else fell away. I didn't answer the phone in those three hours. I should've extended that to being with Kyle—and yet I didn't. Not even for five minutes.

What the hell was wrong with me?

Arriving at the arena for the skills competition, I flipped the phone to Do Not Disturb. The only people who could get through that barrier were my parents, and they wouldn't call.

My parents.

Despite how much they worked—and I worked as a teenager—they made time for things they deemed impor-tant. There was always a meal a week we'd shared together —usually Sunday breakfast before church. At least one of them had always shown up for school things—conference, science fair, graduation.

Tamara—going all the way back to when I was a senior and working myself sick on a final project—wanted me to find more balance and maybe even a boyfriend. Balance hadn't really existed for my parents because they'd always worried about money.

"Mr. Murray?" I turned and the Detroit PR guy—what was his name?—came down the stairs. This needed to be quick. The fastest skater competition started in a few minutes. I wouldn't miss that. "Do you mind if we talk for a quick minute? I'd love to highlight you on Instagram."

Normally, I wanted to be prepared if I had to do anything for the media. Speaking wasn't my strong suit, but I could pull it together when I had too and if I rehearsed. But doing this would get a mention of the company out there and that couldn't hurt.

"Um. Okay. Sure. What did you have in mind? I just don't want to, um, miss the next event."

"It'll be super quick. We can do it right here and use the rink as the background."

I stood and remembered my super casual attire—Detroit sweatshirt with Kyle's number on the back and jeans. Not exactly camera-ready. But I represented the team today, and maybe that was better as a local CEO who was also a major fan.

"Hello again from the All-Star Skills Competition. We're just a few minutes away from the fastest skater competition where we hope to see our own Kyle Pressgrove take the win. I'm with Austin Murray, CEO of Austin Murray Digital Design. What are you looking forward to this weekend?"

I decided to split my focus between David and the camera, which was held by someone David hadn't introduced. I swallowed the nerves that rattled through me anytime I did something like this and dove in. "With the All-Star Game this close to Detroit, I couldn't resist coming down and cheering on our home team. Of course the All-Star Game is such an elite game, and I'm looking forward to the high level of hockey."

"And how do you feel about the Arsenal's chances for playoffs this year?"

"They're looking good. If they keep grinding out these well-played games, I expect us to be in great shape for the post-season. There's nothing better than watching playoff hockey, especially at home, so I'm hoping for a long postseason."

The announcer said the skating competition was about to begin and explained how it worked. I kept myself from turning back to the ice, just in case David tossed out another question.

"Thank you, Austin, for taking a couple of minutes. We'll let you settle in to cheer Kyle on."

"Thank you." I held my smile until the phone lowered.

"Thanks again." David was ridiculously cheerful. He probably had to be for his job. I had to stop myself from taking a step back because of the intensity. "I'll see you at the auction later."

We nodded, and he bounded up the stairs with his assistant. I turned back to the ice and sat just as the skaters were introduced.

My voice grew hoarse from cheering as Kyle's name was called, prompting some sideways glances from the guy that sat on my right. I didn't care; I was a fan, and I wanted the world to know.

Gameplay was fast, but it was nothing compared to the speed these guys shot around the rink. Each skater started at the far edge of the oval, and there were cones and tires set out at the corners to mark the lane. With nothing in the way —no puck to manage or defensemen to dodge—the skaters went all out.

Was there a world record for things like this? How did they compare to speed skaters? That was something to Google later.

Kyle went fourth among eight competitors. He looked relaxed but intense as he set himself at the start line. The scoreboard screen showed him up close, and since he didn't wear a helmet, I appreciated his handsome, determined face.

His feet were in constant motion once he started. It was a wonder, given how far he leaned over in the corners, that he didn't wipe out—the skater from Carolina actually had. Kyle finished in 13.378 seconds, putting him into the lead.

Kyle held the lead until the final skater, who made the

loop in 1 3.3 1 0. He'd lost by the tiniest margin. Despite that, he gave a fist pump into the air and gave the Edmonton player a clap on the back. Both guys beamed. Of course, in a competition where the gap between first and last place was less than a second and a quarter, second place was damn good.

Having seen a bit of Kyle's personality for myself, the happiness didn't come as a surprise. He always had it in interviews, but he had it in person too. A bit of a sheepish-ness sometimes, but always positive.

There was another hour to go of the skills competition, and then it would be back to the hotel to wait for the auction to begin.

A flutter of nerves bubbled up in my chest. I managed to not sound too skittish last night, but could I do it for an entire date?

What if we clicked? Could I find the courage to ask to see him again? Would he be open to that? I knew he was gay, but am I his type? Physically, he more than fit my ideal, and so far, his personality was a winner. He seemed much the same kind, confident guy he was in high school.

He also worked hard, and that meshed with me too. Obviously, he had practices and quite a bit of travel during the months-long hockey season. What did he even get up to during the summer?

I shook my head and pushed my glasses up. This was a ridiculous train of thought. I had no time for a relationship. Hell, even if I had time, I didn't really know how to have one—the hazards of being a controlling workaholic.

Deciding what our auction date could be should be my focus, not thinking about a second one.

The options were many, but I wanted to make sure to do something we'd both like. Technically, the dates were supposed to happen Saturday night after the game or Sunday while everyone was still in Chicago. My flight didn't go out until Sunday night, so we had a bit of time.

The nerves tried to flare up once more, but I tamped them down. No matter what happened, I'd get to enjoy some time with my favorite player.

# FIVE

## KYLE

As IF I wasn't nervous enough, the pushing and shoving backstage didn't help. I don't know what happened with Layne, but trying to keep a hockey player from going off on somebody is never easy—even more difficult when you're not supposed to mess up how you look.

Just one more thing in a surreal day where I skated my ass off in an arena full of people and a nationwide TV audience. The whole event shot by, and I had a blast. A couple of hours later, I couldn't contain my giddiness. Yes, I lost. But I had no more speed to give, so I had nothing to regret.

Mom had hugged me so hard when I caught up with her and Bobby afterward. She didn't even let Bobby mess with me about just barely losing.

Thank God this event was sold out. Mom had tried to get Bobby to bring her along as they were leaving. I couldn't handle Mom watching—it'd be too weird.

Since Layne dropped out after the altercation, I ended up going on sooner—only by five minutes, but it still amped my anxiety about a million times higher. The speed of my heart confirmed that.

The place looked jammed to capacity as I walked out. At least on the stage I didn't have the press of the crowd against me. We should've rehearsed with the frenzy of the cheering people and super loud music. It was all much closer in this small space than in a large arena.

After brunch, I'd snagged Bobby and Sebastian to figure out my walk. They'd agreed I should think James Bond suave with a wide smile and as much warmth as I could muster. Thankfully, Sebastian explained that the Pressgrove brothers' smiles could win over anyone. He went on to do a couple of walks that looked good on him and then I'd tried.

Bobby had snickered, but at least they'd given me something I didn't feel too self-conscious about doing. It'd been a major relief they decided I didn't have to groove in any way.

I second guessed everything as I waited in the wings.

"And here we have Kyle Pressgrove from the Detroit Arsenal." The emcee, Booker Blake, gave me my cue. G gave me one last bit of encouragement from our place backstage.

I strode to the middle of the stage, turned to the crowd, held it for a moment, and then put my James Bond strut or swagger—Bobby and Seb couldn't decide what to call it—to work to travel the catwalk. Booker kept talking. I tried not to focus too much on what he said in case he said something embarrassing.

"You know this guy's got good stamina because he's here and smiling after nearly winning the fastest skater competition. It means he'll be an energetic date."

And then I paid too much attention. Heat rose in my cheeks—the last thing I needed.

I turned twice, slowly, trying to make eye contact with some of the guys as I did. Bobby said the more I connected, the better the bids. I unbuttoned my jacket, dropped my hands to my sides, and hoped I had the look Bobby wanted. I couldn't find him to get any sign.

"We'll start the bidding at the minimum one hundred dollars. Who wants a date with this power forward?"

*Someone make him stop.*

Several paddles went up, and I tried to not look too shocked. I worried about getting one, but this many ratcheted my embarrassment further. A bright red face was not a winning trait.

"Come on, Kyle, move around. Let everybody see what they're bidding on," Booker chided me.

I'd planned to stay right at the end of the walkway, focusing on some of the guys as they bid. I wish I'd paid attention to what other people had done.

I moved though because I didn't want to give Booker the opportunity to pick on me. The guy had been an amazing player but his tendency for biting remarks and trash talk was legendary.

There were people pressed against the catwalk, some holding hands up, and I shook a few, fist bumped others.

"Who wants to go to two hundred?"

Were there even more paddles this time? I wasn't sure.

"Let's go three hundred."

Slightly fewer went up.

Good. The sooner we got down to one, the sooner I'd be allowed to leave the stage.

"How about four?"

That whittled it down to five. I finally found Bobby and Seb, sitting along the wall, and I got a thumbs up. That relaxed me a bit.

Thank God Mom didn't come.

And thank God Bobby didn't have his phone out filming. It'd be bad enough if David streamed it for the team.

"Five hundred?"

One dropped out. Damn. How much were people willing to lay out for a date? Charity sure, but five hundred?

"Remember there are more guys coming up, so if this gets too rich for your blood, you'll have other opportunities to nab a hockey player. Who's got five fifty?"

Only two went for that.

I moved back to the end of the catwalk, and Booker joined me. One paddle belonged to an older gentleman who seemed to be egged on by two friends. The other bidder...

Holy shit.

Austin.

Why would he bid on me? Sure, we'd hung out yesterday—at least until he'd decided a call was more important.

"Seven fifty?"

Wait. What?

I needed to pay attention. Both paddles acknowledged that increase.

"You know I'm not the guy on the ESPN cover, right?" Thankfully that got some laughs and helped break my anxiety.

"Nine hundred," Austin shouted out as he held his paddle higher.

"Yeah, Kyle! Go, man." G's voice rose over the din of the crowd as he called out from backstage.

I fought the urge to bury my face in my hands. The blush became uncontrollable. I got no relief from Bobby or Seb, who just smiled and nodded excitedly.

"Okay, we got nine hundred over here." Booker pointed toward Austin.

The other bidder talked with his friends—a lot. Reading expressions from this distance was difficult, especially with the lights constantly moving over the audience.

He raised his paddle high and shouted, "Nine fifty."

"How about that. A bidding war. Can we get a thousand dollars for this speedy hotshot?" Booker waved his hand next to me as if I was a letter for Vanna White to turn.

"Eleven hundred." Austin again.

Waves of nervousness radiated out from my chest. I contained shudders as best as I could. Not much rattled me, but man, I'd never experienced anything like this before.

"Twelve hundred." The other bidder didn't relent.

The crowd cheered.

This was crazy. Great for the charity though.

"Fifteen hundred." Austin sounded defiant.

With the money he must make, could anyone in this room beat him?

The men conferred again, and one seemed to be emphatically trying to make a point. Whether it was to bid or not bid wasn't clear.

"I've got fifteen hundred for Kyle Pressgrove, number forty-two for the Detroit Arsenal. I need at least fifteen fifty to continue."

I looked around and tried to give a nonchalant shrug before focusing on the bidder with a choice to make. I shot him a questioning look as I pointed between the two of us.

Why not have a little fun with it instead of standing here stressed?

He stared at me, and I thought he might go for more.

"That's fifteen hundred going once."

Yes! The countdown to the end.

More discussion.

"Going twice."

The guy shook his head and put the paddle behind his back as if to stop himself from raising it.

"Sold! To paddle number two forty-one. Congratulations."

I pointed to Austin and gave my widest smile. He smiled back and nodded. Hanging with the hometown guy. That'd be cool.

Everybody applauded and whistled while I took a bow.

Booker stopped my departure, grabbing my arm. "How's it feel to have that little bidding war?"

Here we go. I didn't want to talk. What was I supposed to say?

"Kind of weird, to be honest. I'd hoped I'd be able to get some money to Hockey Allies, but I never imagined this. I appreciate it, and I know Hockey Allies does too. In fact, I'm going to double that final bid to support them even more."

The audience loved that. I'm glad I thought of it. All the guys should do the same. Maybe some would follow my lead.

"That's excellent, Kyle. Thank you on behalf of Hockey Allies. Now go meet your date, and we'll see if anyone else can top your bid. Let's bring out Slater Knox!"

# SIX

## AUSTIN

Holy shit.

I did it.

I'm committed now to hang out with my favorite hockey player for at least an hour.

I attend all kinds of meetings and dinners, but this has me more jittery than any business meeting.

I'd leave the phone off too. The world won't fall apart if I'm not reachable for an hour... hopefully.

Making my way to the cashier to pay up, several people congratulated me, shook my hand, and wished me well on the date. I just smiled and nodded.

Thankfully, the cashier was stationed in the lobby just outside of the ballroom, so the noise dropped to a bearable level.

The guy who kept the bidding going came up next to me and stepped in front of me, friends at his sides, before I'd reached my destination. "Congrats. I so badly wanted to bid more. Luckily, this one talked sense into me because the other one was going to let me keep going. I'm Tom."

We shook hands as we finished introductions. "No hard feelings then?"

"Noooo." The length of the word added to how happy he was to have been stopped. "Spending that much would've been ridiculous, although maybe worth it to sit across the table from Kyle and look at his dreamy face."

"I'm not going to need to separate you two, am I?" Kyle arrived with a charming smile that made my insides quiver in the best way.

"Nah," Tom said. "Just congratulating Austin." He regarded Kyle for a moment that threatened to become awkward because of the silence. "Could I maybe get a selfie with you to mark the event?"

"Of course. As long as the winner doesn't mind." Kyle winked at me, as if I might actually object.

"Sure. I'll even take it."

Tom handed over his phone, and I snapped a couple.

"Hey, perfect." David showed up with his phone in hand. "Can I get a couple with the three of you? Kyle with the guys who battled over him."

The briefest flash of irritation crossed Kyle's eyes, and then it was gone. I hoped I hadn't done something wrong.

"If these guys are okay with it," Kyle said.

Neither of us minded, and David put Kyle between us. The woodsy cologne Kyle wore filled my nostrils, and I subtly breathed in deeply to ensure I'd remember it. Did I miss that yesterday or was it just for the event?

Kyle held us close, arms across our shoulders. I focused on smiling as the warmth of his hand cut right through my light sports coat. He exuded energy and warmth, and combined with his wonderful smell, I was a little lightheaded.

After the photos, Kyle signed Tom's auction program

before Tom disappeared back into the crowd with his friends. David took another couple of pictures of just me and Kyle to commemorate my winning bid, and then he left us alone.

"Congratulations, Austin. Wow. I had no idea when you said you'd be at the auction that you'd do that. Thank you for putting so much into the charity. That was incredible."

"Um.... Well... It's the least I can do for my favorite player." Nervous laughter escaped before I could stop it. I tried to turn it into a groan. "I sound like such a fanboy now. I suppose I should pay so they don't think I tried to run off with you."

His sweet smile reappeared, even bigger. "I'll come with you so I can get those matching funds in. I'm guessing you already have game tickets for tomorrow, perhaps better ones than the suite for the auction winners."

"Yeah." I could do better than one-word answers. Luckily, I found some quick. "I'm not a fan of the suites. I only use our sponsor access to one if I need to impress clients. I prefer to sit in the crowd, which is where I'll be tomorrow."

"I'm the same. The suites are too closed off from the energy."

"Exactly."

I didn't encounter many people who felt the same way I did. Most thought the suite was swanky. Sure there was food and a bar and stuff, but I'd take a good seat in the crowd anytime.

We got in line at the cashier.

I couldn't remember ever having this kind of feeling over a guy. Being near him got my heart racing, set off some butterflies, and made it more difficult for me to form words than I usually did in social settings. It wasn't nerves, although I had that too—but the good feelings outweighed everything else.

Since college, Tamara periodically encouraged me to get out and try to find somebody even though it didn't rank high on my to-do list. Getting all into a guy I'd only see this weekend wasn't ideal for a number of reasons.

As Kyle handed over his credit card to make his donation, I took the moment to study him up close and once again admired how he looked in the suit. It fit just right everywhere—accentuating his broad shoulders, and the shirt fit close enough, I imagined strong pecs. The coat was at the right level where I could admire the lower half of his ass too. I admit I'd kept up with Kyle's online pictures to see if he ever showed much skin.

He didn't.

While some may go shirtless—or guys like Garrett end up the cover guy for ESPN's body issue—Kyle kept it modest.

"Hey, where'd you go?" Kyle flashed that smile again and stepped aside so I could get to the counter.

I'd zoned out thinking about his body. Not good. Shouldn't be going there. Especially around him.

I stepped up, handed over my card, and filled out the auction info.

"Hey bro, you had that walk down perfect, and damn what an amazing bid. Super cool of you to match too."

"Thanks."

Kyle mentioned his brother yesterday. I turned to say hello as I continued to fill out info on the tablet I'd been given.

"Bobby, this is Austin Murray, the guy who, for some reason, decided I was worth all that money." Kyle's bit of self-deprecation added still more to his charm. "He's also one of the team sponsors and is in town for the game. Austin, this is Bobby."

I held my hand out to Bobby, and we traded shakes.

"It's cool you're from Detroit. If the date goes well, maybe you guys can keep seeing each other."

Bobby had the same thought I did, so maybe it wasn't so weird after all. Kyle elbowed his sibling and shot him a death glare. Bobby laughed it off.

"Excuse him, he's got no filter and no sense." Kyle sounded mortified. "Dude, this guy's a sponsor. Don't piss him off."

Bobby's laugh continued, and I joined in, if only to let Kyle know I didn't mind. "It's all right. I'm already a fan so..."

Crap. I ran out of words.

"Austin, nice to meet you. Please go do something fun together." His phone buzzed in his hand, and he stole a look at the screen. "I gotta go. Seb just pulled the car up. See you at the game tomorrow, bro."

The brothers hugged, Bobby said goodbye to me, and then headed out.

"Family. Sometimes, I swear..." He didn't finish the thought, but his tone proved that Bobby had amused him more than annoyed him. "So, do you want to get a drink and watch all this lunacy or..."

The crowd hadn't gotten any quieter as the bachelors continued to take the stage. What did I want to do? I hadn't expected to need a plan to hang out with Kyle until tomorrow or Sunday.

"I wouldn't mind staying out of the ballroom for a little longer. All this loudness in a small space is more than I'm used to."

39

"Works for me." Kyle looked beyond me. "How about we go back over to the bar? Looks a lot less crowded there."

"Great." We crossed the lobby. "Did you have fun with the speed competition? It was super fun to watch, cheering you on."

"I don't really have words. Being here is major. I wanted this since I was a kid—to be an All-Star. Now I can check that off along with a Winter Classic. Hopefully, there's a Stanley Cup in my future. Just being on the ice this afternoon with those guys was epic. I tried to explain to my mom why I wasn't disappointed that I didn't win this afternoon. To compete with those guys—the very fastest in the league —was a win."

In the bar, Kyle guided us to a table that would be out of view of anyone coming or going from the auction.

"And tomorrow is just gonna be a big game of pickup," he continued. "Sure, there's competition, but the All-Star Game is unlike anything else. Winter Classics are cool, but those are serious games that affect stats. Tomorrow is a bunch of guys who don't usually get to play together having a great time. God, I'm babbling."

Excitement flowed off him—in his voice and the animated way he moved his hands around. It totally charmed me.

"I totally get it. I mean, I always want to win in business, but sometimes it's just the people you're around. I imagine it's like being invited to speak on a panel and the other panelists are people I highly admire, and I'm honored to be in their company."

"Exactly!"

We paused to give a drink order—same as last night, bourbon for me and ginger ale for him. Then I said, "So, tomorrow. What are you thinking? We could keep it as simple as dinner or something different. How tired will you be after the game?"

"Between the afternoon timing of the game and the postgame adrenaline, I'll be good into the evening. Plus I'm here on Sunday, and other than brunch with my family mid-morning, I'm free, and I'll probably spend any free time with Bobby."

Interesting. I planned to head home Sunday night so I'd be in the office first thing Monday, so something during the day on Sunday. I hadn't thought of anything particularly creative for our date though—I kept landing back on dinner. I'd had my assistant, Jack, find some good places, so I put forward one of those.

Just as we settled on the place for dinner after the game, Kyle and I both got texts at the same time. Someone decided they needed a picture of all the bachelors and their dates.

At least we had the date scheduled.

Now I could just be nervous about the actual date rather than it's planning.

# SEVEN

## KYLE

WHAT A DAY!

My first All-Star Game.

My first All-Star Game with a goal.

My first All-Star Game with my brother and mom in the audience.

I got the goal on a sweet two-on-one as me and Kingsbury took off on a breakaway. Despite the fact we'd only played together in this game, we read each other perfectly and we messed that defenseman in front of us relentlessly. Kingsbury pulled the D way out of position, and I slammed the puck home.

I don't keep many of my highlights, but I'd talk to our press office to get video of this goal for a souvenir. I had the clip of my first NHL goal too, and Mom had a ton of stuff she shot before I got to college.

Mom beamed so much when I saw her and Bobby after the game. She was always so proud of me, and this time out, I was proud I'd been able to do that with her right there in the arena.

Sadness washed over me once they'd left, and thankfully it had waited. I thought of Dad a lot, even though he'd been gone now nearly twenty years. He'd supported my early playing years as much as Mom had, and I had no doubt if he were alive, he'd have been here too. The major career milestones, like today, were always a bittersweet flavor without him here too.

I shook off those thoughts as I checked my watch. Austin was fifteen minutes late and not even a text message.

I'd arrived early at the restaurant he'd picked because things wrapped up at the arena sooner than expected. I'd given myself some buffer in our plans in case I got stuck there longer. I hated being late. Dad always said that one of the measures of a good person was punctuality. Being late equaled disrespect, especially if there was no advanced noticed.

Everything had seemed good earlier. I'd texted him before I'd headed here, and he'd sent a thumbs up back, so it'd seemed like all was good.

"Can I get food here? And take it to the table when my date shows up?" I looked to the bartender who was topping off a drink at one of the taps. I hadn't grabbed any of the food before I left, and that'd been a mistake. My stomach rumbled, demanding refueling.

"Of course." He turned to the counter behind him, grabbed a menu, and handed it to me. "Get you anything else to drink while you look that over?"

I'd been chugging water so far to rehydrate, but with no game or practice tomorrow, I could go for something more, especially with food on the way. "I'll take whatever local beer you recommend."

"Cool. Back with that in a minute."

"Kyle, I'm so sorry." I looked up from the menu and

found Austin coming toward me. "I ended up taking a call in the arena parking lot and lost track of time. I should've at least been driving this direction while I talked."

He looked so distraught that I couldn't be mad. He certainly had a knack for being glued to his phone though. Plenty of people lived on their phones. I certainly got caught up in mine sometimes—especially traveling. But I tried to never let it interfere. I guessed he couldn't get away from it being a CEO. Still, it kinda sucked.

"Here's your beer." The bartender set a tall glass down filled with a dark amber liquid. I had a good idea I'd like that. "I got you an Anti-Hero. It's a favorite of mine. If you don't like it, let me know and I can get you something else. Are you ready to order?"

I took a drink.

"This is damn good. Thank you." I looked to Austin. "I think we're ready to sit down. I can close this out with you." I reached for my wallet.

"No worries." The bartender waved me off. "I'll find out your server, and it'll all be on one bill."

I pulled a ten from my wallet and put it on the bar. "That's for you. Thanks for putting this great beer in my hand. Have a good night."

"Thank you, sir." The bartender smiled, and Austin and I headed back to the host stand.

"Oh, man, I'm sorry," Austin said. "I left you here so long you got hungry."

"The hazard of post-game timing; sometimes the hungry comes roaring in faster than I expect."

He sighed as we approached the host stand. "I lose myself in the work sometimes. It's terrible. Tamara, my friend and business partner, calls me out on it sometimes."

The host got us seated quickly. He'd taken my information when I came in, but I hadn't wanted to sit at a table by myself.

"That sounds like something Bobby would do." As we talked, we studied the menu. "He makes no bones, despite being younger, telling me exactly what I might be doing wrong in my life."

"It's good we've got people looking out for us."

He wasn't wrong about that.

"I guess everybody needs that sometimes." I set the menu aside so I could focus on Austin. "Do you really have to be that close to the phone all the time? It seems... exhausting."

"For better or worse, I try to be available anytime someone wants to talk to me. I used to expect the same out of everybody else, but Tamara got me to see that just because *I* wanted to work every hour did not mean that everybody else did or should be expected to. But I never want to be a bottleneck, you know? I don't want someone stuck because I wasn't available."

He talked very softly, and a sadness filled his eyes. I hadn't meant to take us there with the question—instead it was to find out more about him. We didn't have to get into heavy topics. This was supposed to be fun.

The waiter came and we ordered. Despite the fact that my stomach wanted the entire menu, I kept things fairly reasonable with a pasta dish and salad. I had snacks in the room if I needed them later. Austin ordered salmon.

"For what it's worth"—Austin picked up again— "my phone is off. It will not bother us the rest of the evening."

"Cool." Our eyes met, and it was like looking into a kaleidoscope. I hadn't realized before how much energy and attentiveness there was there. He smiled as I looked at him, and his gaze made my heart speed up a notch. Yeah, I knew he was cute, but suddenly, directly across the table from him, I felt a spark I hadn't felt in a very long time.

What did that even mean?

# EIGHT

## AUSTIN

KYLE HAD SLICKED-BACK hair in almost any image I'd ever seen of him. He'd worn his hair that way last night too. Tonight, his bangs fell just the smallest bit over his forehead, and sometimes he'd push them back. No one had asked my opinion—and I didn't verbalize it—but I wanted to see him like this more because it raised his sexy factor several notches more than usual.

His gaze pierced me, scrutinized me, but not in a way that made me uncomfortable. Instead, warm tingles spread from my chest, and it felt good.

If this wasn't the first moments of our first date, I'd try to kiss that smile because it was just that perfect.

I should not be thinking that way!

I restrained from shaking it out of my head because it would look weird to randomly shake my head for no reason. But the desire to kiss him was strong.

My beer came, and I finally had something to do with my hands. I took a drink and a deep breath.

No more thoughts of kissing!

"What turned you into a hockey fan?"

I don't think anyone had ever asked me that. Maybe it's because hockey is such a passion in Michigan, everyone's expected to be into it.

I remembered exactly what it was though.

"When I was six, I saw a bunch of older kids playing on a pond. I only caught a glimpse as we were in the car, but I remember it so well. I was in the backseat, and we drove by a park that had a frozen pond. Those kids zipping back and forth playing looked like they were having so much fun." I smiled at the memory. "After that, I started watching on TV when I could. Neither of my parents liked sports, so I only got to watch when my uncle would take care of me on weekend afternoons while my parents worked. He was a big Arsenal fan."

Kyle's full attention was fixed on me. I needed this skill, even now I struggled to not look elsewhere. The intimacy of this quiet, personal dinner conversation thrilled and scared me in equal measures. I didn't usually interact with people this way.

"Did you ever play?"

"No." I sighed. "I stood on skates once at a birthday party. Some kid I sorta knew from my sixth-grade class invited everybody to a skate party. My coordination was not great, and I ended up traumatized by my klutziness. Even if I'd managed to skate, there's no way my parents could've afforded the gear."

Kyle nodded. "Yeah, I always got an earful when I grew so much that I had to get new gear more than once a season. It was good-natured, and my parents totally supported me, but hockey is so expensive. I tried to soften the blow by reminding them that at least I wasn't a goalie."

More laughter. I enjoyed the warm, bass timbre from him. It reverberated through me.

The server placed the appetizer on the table, and Kyle immediately nabbed half of the chicken skewers. He bit off some chicken and then shot me a sheepish look as he realized that he looked like a crazed man who hadn't seen food in weeks.

"No worries. I kept you waiting after all, so get that postgame hunger fed." I grabbed one of the skewers and got my first bite in the time that he nearly devoured his first stick. "You know, we went to the same high school. I saw you play a lot. Even then, I thought it was obvious you'd make it to the pros. It's been so cool following you all these years."

Even in the subdued light of the restaurant, I could see his cheeks pink up.

"What?" I asked, wondering what could've embarrassed him about his high school career.

"Oh wow. We went to school together. Why didn't you tell me that yesterday?"

I shrugged.

"This is gonna sound so, I don't know, conceded or something." Kyle pushed his bangs back again. Could I maneuver the date so we get to the point where I can run my hand through his hair? I doubt I have the skills for that. "My mom has a lot of footage of me from high school. I had to look at it a couple years ago to find some footage for the Arsenal's social media team. I looked so gangly. I seemed on the verge of losing control and falling over. I'm so much more confident now. I don't know. Kinda silly, right?"

Good humor danced around his face and shown in his eyes. He had to have been replaying the footage in his head.

"I never thought you looked anything but perfect." Perfect? Really? I had to pick that word? "But of course you skate different and better now." I pushed on, hoping to not sound too obsessed. "You've been coached for years, and you certainly have filled out and got stronger since your Fincher High days."

I had a picture of him somewhere that I snapped of him standing around during warm-ups before one game after I'd discovered how insanely hot he was. His helmet was off, and he stood with one of his line mates. There was laughter and joy on his face much like I'd seen after the skills competition. The term *gangly* never entered my mind when I saw him around school either.

Kyle took a moment to focus on his food instead of me. "I appreciate you saying that." He looked back with a super shy smile before redirecting our conversation. "So you've never tried skating again? The Arsenal has days season-ticket holders and sponsors come skate with us. You should totally do that."

"That's kind of a bucket list thing I'd have to work up the nerve to do. Not being able to afford sports as a kid is why I set up a foundation to fund after school sports programs. I'd like to help make sure kids who want to play can, regardless of the family's financial situation."

Kyle nodded as his face lit up. "I work with organizations like that as often as I can. I was lucky my parents were supportive and had the money."

The server returned with salads, and Kyle looked contemplative as the plates were set, and we both had fresh pepper added to our greens.

"Did you say you're here tomorrow?" Kyle asked, a tinge of excitement in his voice.

I nodded. "My flight's not until seven."

He reached into the pocket inside his jacket and pulled out his phone. A mischievous glint danced in his eyes as he typed.

"What're you up to?"

He wouldn't do anything too crazy, would he? Nerves pulsed through me as I tried to guess.

"If I can make the arrangements, tomorrow we skate."

Was he serious? He wanted to do more than just dinner? He wants to skate with me?

Oh my God.

# NINE

## KYLE

WHOA.

Austin greeted me with a crooked smile as I entered the rink.

Honestly, I expected another late showing.

The pristine sheen of the ice indicated he hadn't been out there yet. He bobbled just a little bit as I approached. Austin radiated determination as he deliberately took measured steps. Walking in skates took some getting used to.

"Laced up, ready to go." I called out. "Great!"

He shrugged, and we traded a quick hug hello. We'd hugged goodbye last night too, and he felt good. Honestly, I would've hugged longer if the Lyft hadn't arrived. He fit against me so well.

This embrace felt right. I hated that I carried my skates in my left hand, so I couldn't hold him as tightly as I wanted.

"I wanted to get here on time and get into the skates to see how they felt." He indicated the skates I held. "Do you

55

take skates everywhere you go? I would've thought your gear was on its way back."

"I keep gear at Bobby's, so when I'm in town, we can easily play pickup. And I'm super picky about my skates anyway. Total custom fit."

"Oh, nice. Kinda sounds like a spy though—having gear stashed around."

I smirked up to him. "Shhhh. Don't give away my secret."

We held that look for a moment before I sat on the first row of bleachers. I pulled off my sneakers, pulled on the skates, and started lacing.

"Was your brunch good?"

"Yeah." I looked up as I finished one skate and moved to the other. "Good food, good chat. I love hanging with my family anytime I can. Bobby and Seb took Mom to the airport, and I came here."

"I hope this didn't take you away from them." Guilt crept into his voice.

"Not at all." I stood and stamped my feet a couple of times to make sure my feet were set right.

"Damn, you're fast. It took me a few minutes to get the laces right."

"I could do this with my eyes closed I think."

Austin fidgeted with just a bit of fear in his eyes

"I promise this will be good. Fun." I gestured for him to step onto the ice. I followed close behind, just in case he needed an assist.

He hesitated, looking at the ice as if it might come alive and swallow him up. I didn't want to make it a big deal, so I stepped out and faced him.

I held out my hand.

He took in a deep breath before he grabbed on and squeezed it tighter than I'd expected.

"Are you sure this is okay? We're taking up an entire rink for me to repeatedly fall on my ass."

Austin stood between me and the boards, keeping his grip on me and using his other hand to steady himself on the ledge. His concentration... I kind of wanted to kiss the crinkles along his forehead and around his eyes.

"Totally fine. We've got this rink for ninety minutes. This is where Bobby plays, and he helped me get it."

"How'd I let you talk me into this?"

"That's not how I recall it." I slowly moved us along, trying to take his mind off the mechanics of how he moved. "You were pretty excited about the idea."

"Too many beers maybe?"

"Nah. Not with just the one." I smiled, and some of the fear left his eyes.

He took his hand from mine and attached it firmly to my forearm—like an action figure that had super powered grip. It didn't hurt through my hoodie and sweatshirt, and honestly, I kind of liked how he took charge and held me how he wanted.

"Now we're going to glide away from the boards. You're gonna trust me. I won't let you fall. Once you lose the fear of getting hurt, you'll enjoy this more." I sent him all the confident energy I had. "Trust me?"

"Yes." He didn't pause to think. "You coach kids. I should be able to do this."

I nodded. "You *can* do this."

His hold relaxed just a bit.

"Now, let me go." He hesitantly released me, and I waited patiently so we didn't move too fast. "Now I'm going to come around in front of you." I easily pivoted so we stood face-to-face. "Now, bend your legs just a little." I squatted a bit—exaggerating my normal stance—to demonstrate. "It's like you're about to sit. That lowers your center of gravity. Now just walk forward, one skate in front of the other."

He made tentative steps, and I stepped back to mirror him. It only took a few more steps before he glided more than walked. Exactly what he should do.

"See. Progress. Now think about this like it's a dance. You'll mirror the moves I make. We'll go as slow or fast as you want."

Austin vibrated, his shudders rolling into my hands and arms. I couldn't tell if it was from fear or the insta-bility in his strides. My grip on his wrists was firm but not tight.

"Try not to look down at what your feet are doing. You'll tend to move the direction your eyes go. My young students are the same—always wanting to look at their feet or the puck. Keep your head up."

His strides improved as we started a second lap with his speed increasing too.

"Holy shit." His eyes were wide and happy. I'm doing it." Laughter and joy filled his voice

"Yeah. Yeah, you are." My chest filled with pride at teaching him. Kids were never scared of skating, and I wasn't used to trying to coach someone who was. "Told you I could get you to skate."

"It doesn't seem nearly as hard as I made it out to be."

We continued to move around the rink.

"Once you've got the basics down, it's like anything else. The bicycle cliché in effect. Of course we still have to get you to stop..."

"Oooh." Now he sounded like one of the kids as they asked about something they really want to do—usually advanced things like slap shots. "Can you teach me to snow somebody?"

I bit back a laugh at his excitement. He had a ways to go before he'd be fast enough and have the blade control to spray snow.

"Now," I said with my stern coaching voice, "I don't want to have to put you in the penalty box for unsportsman-like conduct."

A flash of something went through his eyes that sent warm vibrations through me. What was that? I wanted to see it again.

He hummed in response. The sound went straight to my cock, and it stirred in my sweats.

What the hell?

Yeah, Austin was cute, but it wasn't like we were going to do anything else. I liked him and that I could do this for him.

The slight blush on his cheeks highlighted the moment. Mine were probably the same. Did he feel—

"So, um, how do I stop?"

Good. Back to the lesson.

"My advice for beginners is to snowplow, so you turn both skates out to make a plow." I let him go and skated backward. He continued forward. "I'll skate a few paces away. You keep going and stop before you hit me."

"I don't want to run into you." He wobbled as he said it.

"You're not going to hurt me, and I'll catch you if something goes wrong."

I sprinted, skating backward as his forward momentum continued. I put about twenty-five feet between us. His form had already improved in just the short time we'd been here.

"As you turn your skates out, make sure you dig in to

stop."

It only took a few seconds before he did run into me. I caught him as his skates pivoted weird. Thankfully, he didn't panic, and he used me for stability as he brought his skates firmly under him.

"Sorry."

I didn't mind his body running into me—at all.

"No worries. We'll work on that. The point of today was to get you moving, to give you what you didn't get at that party. Few things make me happier than skating around to some music."

I pulled out my phone, turned up the volume, and started my playlist. There was enough sound with it in my hoodie pocket so we could hear.

"Seriously?" A big grin was on his face. "We get to skate to Madonna?"

"Well, it's an eclectic playlist, but yeah... skate to some music." My suggestion had exactly the impact I hoped. I hated it when people missed out on experiences, and I was glad to give him this one. "So, you want to know a secret?"

"Of course."

Instead of continuing to go backward, I skated alongside Austin, letting him hold onto my arm again. While I swayed to the music, I made sure it wasn't enough to knock him off course or balance.

"I always have this playlist with me. It's dance music for the most part but some songs are slower. I always start with this one because I saw a live video of Madonna in concert doing it with all these roller skater dancers. I love the disco vibe, and it's a great remix of music.'"

I subtly sped us up. He kept up. I suspected the music kept him from overthinking the skating.

"You carry your own skating music?"

"Totally. It's not too weird, right?"

"Not at all. I like knowing this about you. And this is a great version of this song. I'll have to check out the video sometime."

"You could just pull out your phone now and look?" I couldn't help myself, poking a bit at his phone issue.

"My phone is in my shoe. When I talked to Tamara this morning, she actually ordered me to leave the phone off. I wouldn't be surprised if she calls a couple times just to make sure I don't pick up."

"She sounds awesome."

"I'm lucky she tries so hard. I'm not an easy person to change. It's just..."

I waited to see if he was going to continue, but eventually I nudged. "You can say whatever. I've already shared a secret playlist after all."

"My parents worked hard and never had much to show for it. They kept food on the table and made sure I did what I needed to do to ensure I'd get through college. Thankfully, I've been able to retire them and make sure they're comfortable. But..."

He looked at me and lost control of his strides. I kept him steady and slowed us down.

"Sorry." He looked at me with sad eyes, the same ones I'd gotten a flash of last night.

I slowed us more.

"Maybe I'm shouldn't skate and talk?"

I raised an eyebrow in questioning surprise. "You know that's a little ridiculous, right? I mean, we scream across the ice at each other all the time."

"I know." He grinned, his mood lifting a bit. He pointed forward with his free hand. "Let's speed up again. I have to admit that was fun."

I nodded and gently ratcheted up our speed, bringing it back to where it'd been.

"This must be boring after the speed from the skills competition."

"Never. Any skate is a good skate. I love it when we do the open skate events. You really should come. It's such a good time."

It'd be cool to skate more with Austin. I liked being around him—easy to talk to, good looking, plus that something that got me excited in a way that I hadn't ever been.

"My parents always worked." He didn't look at me this time, and his voice was more monotone than before. "Sometimes more than one job each. I made money where I could. They never wanted to run the risk of losing the house or whatever. They'll never be without though. The key patent for the technology AMDD developed is jointly in their name, and that should keep them taken care of."

It didn't seem like he'd finished, so I stayed quiet. I'd give him all the time he needed to either continue or change the topic.

"Even with that, I always think in the back of my head when I don't answer a call that it's going to fuck everything up, and I'll lose it all. It doesn't matter there's an entire staff backing me up. I've even tried therapy, and I can't totally push away these feelings."

We kept skating, and he settled into good strides. He seemed to be holding something back, but it didn't seem right to question him on something so personal.

"Kind of lame, huh?" He looked to me and didn't stumble.

"Not at all. I totally get how lessons from parents stick with you."

# TEN

## AUSITN

FEW PEOPLE KNEW the story of my parents. Tamara and maybe two or three others. I'm not sure what inspired me to tell Kyle. I felt comfortable around him, though, in a way I'm not with most people. He's got a bit of a jock swagger and confidence, but he's really just open, kind, and a nice guy. Somehow, he quieted some of the voices in my head that pushed me to always be doing something related to work.

"I get how taking care of family is important." Kyle spoke softly, and I paid close attention to make sure I heard him over the music. "My dad taught me to skate when I was four. Took me to my first hockey game that year too. By five, I'd joined a mites team. Bobby started playing at five too, but I had the aptitude for it and moved on to more competitive teams. Mom and Dad supported me every step of the way."

The wistful quality of his voice captured me. It couldn't get more perfect than hearing a story about skating while we were going around the ice. I hoped I wouldn't screw up the mood with a klutzy moment.

"When I was eight, Dad died in a car accident while he was on a business trip to London."

Involuntarily, I gripped Kyle's hand tighter. He didn't flinch. "I'm so sorry."

"Thank you." His smile was the kindest I'd ever seen—the simplicity of it said everything was okay. "We can consider this the family sharing time of our skate date."

He just called this a date. Did he mean that in the context of the auction win or...?

"After the funeral, my grandpa and uncle told me I was the man of the house. I had to look after Mom and Bobby. I took that very seriously, looking after Bobby at school, trying to help Mom when I saw that she was sad. Grandpa in particular kept reminding me of it until he passed away when I was in high school. Despite what Mom and Bobby have said over the years, it's hard for me to let it go. Family was important already, but this extra layer's been drilled into me. So different circumstances, but we can't shake off what we *learned* as kids."

We'd shared a lot. If we weren't skating, I'd pull him into a hug.

"The weird thing is," I picked up, "they don't get they can finally let go. They still scrimp on food, and I can't convince them that they can buy something just for the hell of it."

"Sounds like they're stuck in their routine just like you and I are. Mom tells me I worry too much and spend too much time keeping tabs on her and Bobby rather than finding someone..."

Uh-oh. What happened?

"I'm totally babbling. Sorry."

I'm not sure who was more vulnerable.

"You should bring your folks to a game sometime." Kyle

moved the conversation as the music coming from his pocket kept playing dance tunes. "Between your sponsor access and what I get as a player, we can set them up great."

"I've tried. They don't want me to spend money. I wish life hadn't been so hard on them that they can't enjoy more now."

Kyle looked at me and again raised that eyebrow, except this time it came with a quirky smile. "Hmmm. That sounds familiar."

"Whoa. That's not fair." I knocked into his shoulder, temporarily forgetting I was on skates. My feet sputtered, but Kyle leaned into me and kept me upright. "And maybe you should take some advice from your mother. Seems like she's in favor of you settling down like Bobby."

He grunted, deep and gravely. What sounds would me make if he were under me? Or over me? Anywhere with me in bed.

Oh, man. We're so far away from that.

I couldn't go there. I'd already thought about that while drifting off to sleep last night, and while it was a sexy, great fantasy, it would never come true.

"I've never figured out how to date and do the travel, the practices, the games, and everything else. How could I give anyone the time they deserved? I know a lot of guys date and get married while playing the game, but I can't imagine being able to make that work."

Kyle and I had unexpected things in common. Our pasts had interesting intersections with family and obligations.

"You're really tight with your family. Has it always been that way?" Probably a weird question to ask, but his family seemed so different than mine.

"Totally." He lit up. "It's all hands on deck for the holidays. Sometimes, I don't get as many days as Mom and Bobby get, but I manage to be home on Christmas Day. The league's good about that, even around prep for the Winter Classic for teams that play in that. Last year, we celebrated here because Bobby and Seb wanted to host at their new place. I expect will be there again soon enough because they want to start a family."

I didn't miss the extra inflection in his voice, and I caught a twinkle "You're looking forward to being an uncle?"

"For sure. Between me and Mom, the kid will be wildly spoiled." Something ran through his mind that I couldn't decipher, but I caught his expression out of the corner of my eye. "They'll be awesome parents too. Sebastian was a perfect match for Bobby."

"Can I ask, did your mom freak out at all when both sons turned out to be gay? Sometimes I think my parents try to forget about it."

Out of nowhere, I realized skating and talking wasn't quite so hard. It became more like driving a car and occasionally glancing at the passenger.

"Mom was always super great. I got outed at thirteen." He laughed even though that sounded horrible. "I got caught at hockey camp with Garrett Howell."

"Whoa!" That was too loud. I darted my eyes around to make sure we were still alone. "Wait. Same guy from the auction and who's on the ESPN cover?"

"The same." The smirk on his face said everything. "G billeted with us when we played juniors. We were horny teenagers who were out to each other. We messed around a lot. We got caught at camp by another kid who decided to freak out."

Kyle told this with amusement in his voice.

"Parents were called. Things were said. We didn't get thrown out, but we were no longer allowed to be in the same bunkhouse. Garrett's my bestie. And Mom was great. She was happy Garrett and I were safely experimenting with each other instead of random people."

Kyle related all this with exaggerated hand gestures, and until he finished, I didn't realize he'd let go of me.

"I would've died if I ever got caught. It stressed me out just hearing the story. Did you and Garrett ever date?"

"Nah. We're too close for that. We even stopped fooling around not too much after we got caught because it started to feel a little weird." He didn't move to retake my hand, and I skated on my own—which I had to not fixate on. "What about you? How'd you come out?"

"For all the time that my parents wanted me to focus on things to earn money, they also wanted me to start dating. I finally came out at sixteen to get them to stop asking about girls. They said all the right things, but there was an undertone of disappointment. I've still never brought anyone home. The few people in college I dated never really clicked anyway."

He nodded and looked a little sad.

"Sorry," I said, anxiousness exploding in my chest. "Too much serious talk." I tried to laugh it off, but even to my ears, it sounded fake and even sadder.

"We've got about twenty minutes before they're gonna kick us out of here. Let's see if we can add to your speed and get you to move to the music." Kyle allowed me to put my discomfort aside by focusing on what we were really here to do. As he'd done earlier, he relaxed me. "What do you think?"

"I trust you to not let me fall on my ass. Let's do it."

# ELEVEN

## KYLE

"LET ME GET THIS STRAIGHT. You want to see Austin again, even though he was late to the first date and he as much as said he had trouble not being completely work focused?"

I misread how Bobby would take the news. Maybe I should have kept the flaws to myself, but I wanted his full opinion.

"I get that he's handsome and totally your type. But I know you. You're not going to tolerate anyone who's so focused on work, especially since you historically have had worries over your own relationship commitments."

Bobby's voice boomed through my car, and I hit the volume on the steering wheel to bring it down. I'd held back calling him immediately after our skate date yesterday because I wanted to think through what I might be signing myself up for. So I'd churned it over on the flight home this morning and through practice. Now, as I drove to Mom's to sign some things she had for a charity auction, it had seemed like a good time to talk.

"He seemed to know it was not good to be late or be on the phone. Our skate outing went perfectly."

"Much as I want you to find someone, this guy hasn't exactly started off on the best foot."

"I'm going to give him a chance, especially now that we're back home. See what happens."

"Where are you guys going?"

Thankfully, he stopped trying to talk me out of having another date. Although if this went south, there'd be an *I told you so* followed by an extensive analysis—the hazard of a brother who'd become a therapist.

"Kennedy's wife is opening her first gallery show next week. The entire team is going." Kennedy captained the team. Adriana, his wife, was a talented artist, and I loved seeing her get the recognition of this show because her work was gorgeous.

"That's good. At least you're doing something a little different from dinner and a movie."

"Exactly. Hang out, maybe talk about art, and who knows what else. Besides, we've already had dinner, so we know what that's like."

"Just make sure to take care of yourself, bro. Don't give this guy your heart until you know he's right for you."

"I don't think anybody's making long-term commitments. But good advice as always."

I might have lied to him.

During the skate, as we talked about our families and childhoods, I saw the possibilities of a relationship. Not only that, I genuinely liked being around him. The opening would allow us to see more of how we meshed, how we did around others, and if he could be on time and attentive.

"Okay, I'm at Mom's. Hope you get home soon."

70

"It ain't looking good man; GPS just added ten minutes."

"Yikes. Alright, I'll let you get back to your audiobook."

"Cool. Take care, bro."

Mom still lived in the house Bobby and I grew up in. She'd done a fair bit of renovation after we moved out—part of which I'd helped pay off a couple of years ago. As she'd rightfully said, she no longer had two kids, so she might as well transform those rooms.

Mine became her home office. Bobby's ended up as the guest room. She's also made over the kitchen into the ultra-modern style she'd always wanted. She loved cooking and had even talked about ditching her work in human resources to become a chef.

Walking in the backdoor to the kitchen, the smell of basil hit me. She had something going, maybe pesto. I called out a hello as I went to peek inside the pots on the stove.

"Kyle. Thanks so much for coming by. I know it's out of your way, but I wanted to get this stuff delivered tomorrow to be photographed for the online catalog."

I inhaled from one of the pots before I turned. It was pesto, one of my favorite things. "Of course." I reached for a spoon, but she slapped away my hand—just like I knew she would.

"Nope. You know better than that." I dropped the spoon back in its holder on the stovetop. I glanced at her with sad eyes. "You are welcome to stay for dinner though if you want."

I smiled and embraced her petite frame. "Hi, Mom. And I'd love to."

I took off my coat and hung it on one of the hooks where our coats had always gone.

As always, Mom looked wonderful. Her black hair,

streaked with gray that she loved, was pulled back in a pony tail as was her preferred style. Her brown eyes carried so much joyful energy—so much so that anytime I was in a bad mood she could lift me right out of it with just a look. She'd been home long enough to not only get things cooking but to change out of her dressy work clothes and into jeans and an Arsenal sweatshirt. I don't think anyone had more Arsenal clothing than she did.

"That's everything on the table. They sent some great stuff as usual. Kennedy's jerseys are going to go for a lot, I think."

She'd set a silver sharpie out, ready for me to get to work. Two sticks, some pucks, and two pairs of gloves waited for me.

"I wish I would be here for the auction to support it even more."

Mom volunteered with a grief counseling organization for nearly twenty years now. They'd helped her when Dad died, and now she worked with others. I made sure to get her anything she needed for fundraisers—whether it was my stuff or other players.

"You've had your share of auctions recently. How was it with that young man? He was quite good-looking from the pictures Bobby shared."

Bobby hadn't mentioned sharing any auction stuff with Mom.

"He sent me the link from Hockey Allies site since you didn't." She threw me a smirk. "I saw the picture on the team Instagram, and you raised a nice amount of money too."

I'd forgotten about David's pictures. "It went pretty good. I think I'm going to ask him out next week. We kind of clicked, so I thought I'd see if he'd want to go out again."

Might as well just put that out there in case Bobby said anything. I could count on him to keep my reservations quiet but not necessarily the date itself.

"That's good; you need to get out more." She busied herself chopping some vegetables she'd pulled from the fridge. "And now that Bobby's all settled, we need to get you married off too."

"Mom! Married off? Really?"

"What? Aren't I allowed to hope for that?"

She was totally pulling my chain, and I loved it. I just shook my head and started signing things, pretending like she wasn't still looking at me with her patented *I know best* grin.

# TWELVE

## AUSTIN

"Sounds like coming back Sunday night was the right choice." Tamara looked pleased as we sat at the conference table in my office. We munched on our favorite club sandwiches from the deli across the street. A dinner meeting to top off the day.

"The weekend was great. The All-Star stuff was .cool. And Kyle..." I took an extra breath as I remembered our time. "Dinner was good, but going skating with him was the best." I thought twice before I spoke again but decided to go for it. "I think I might want to see him again."

Her eyes bugged out, and I think she nearly spit soda as she covered her mouth. "Talk about burying the headline. You couldn't have said that earlier today? That's major. I can't remember the last time you've come close to saying anything like that."

I picked that moment to take a giant bite of sandwich.

I've been afraid to talk about it on the off chance I would jinx the entire idea. I hadn't been this excited about even the potential of a date in a very long time.

"We had bigger things to deal with this morning," I

finally said. "You have no idea—actually, maybe you do— how difficult this is for me to consider. The news that Chevy, our longest and biggest client, now has a former employee running development at our rival makes me want to shelf any idea of having a date. Not to mention tomorrow's presentation..." I sighed.

Tamara put her sandwich down and fixed me with her look of resolve, which she usually pulled out when I was overthinking. "With Chevy, we haven't done anything wrong. I've got lunch tomorrow with some of our key contacts to get a true read on if we need to worry about Carlos in his new position. We've had no issues being in their vehicles, and we've always innovated beyond their expectations. And you said yourself, the team is more than ready for tomorrow based on what you reviewed on the plane last night."

I nodded. I knew all of this. I obsessed anyway. You could never prepare enough. The team didn't need to over prepare, that was a burden I tried to keep for myself whenever possible.

"Have we considered the ramifications if Chevy pulls out? I mean really look at the worst-case scenario to make sure we're ready?" I dove right back in. If I had the data one way or another, it would help me. I ate more as I silently ticked off what I knew. We seemed pretty safe, but I didn't know the ins and outs of every contract anymore because there were so many.

"Certainly the board will get skittish if we lose them because they're the largest." Tamara's tone said she didn't really want to do this, but she'd pacify me. "But we have two model years to make up the shortfall if they exit. I'll get a more in-depth analysis together so we know all the what ifs."

"Thanks. It might be more than we need but better to have it ready." That was my attempt to acknowledge that I might just be asking for too much.

She nodded and finished taking notes before she met my gaze again. "You know, this won't all go away overnight?" She gestured around, indicating the company as a whole.

"I know." And I did. We had issues, but it also wouldn't just collapse. "I just want us to be safe. Make sure everything is buttoned up and everybody's loving what we do."

My phone chirped with a text that I knew came from Kyle. He was only the fourth person to get their own tone on my phone—my parents and Tamara were the others.

The phone sat face down on the tabletop. I usually stole looks at alerts when the screen lit up, but I wanted to be more mindful and not always jump for the phone. It challenged me, especially since I knew Kyle had sent the message. But I needed to practice.

"You're not going to check?" She eyed me suspiciously.

"An exercise in self-control."

She opened her mouth, then closed it and then looked thoroughly confused. I held back a laugh. "Are you some kind of doppelgänger?" What I couldn't keep down was a silly smile. "There's more going on than you've told me isn't there? Who knew you even had a dopey grin like that. I quite like it. Don't let him get away. Check that message."

"Only if you tell him that you made me look."

*Hey Austin. Hope it's okay I'm texting. Just wanted to wish you good luck with the presentation tomorrow.*

A giddy feeling washed over me. Should I even have that as an adult? Seemed like it should be more of a teenager thing. He'd only wished me good luck.

I typed: *Thanks! We're as ready as we're going to be. How was practice today?*

*Practice was good. Already eager to play Thursday night.*

I sent the text and then started another: *And just so you know, when you texted I had my phone face down on the table. Tamara insisted that I turn it over to see what you said. So I am pouncing on every single message.* I finished with a smiley face emoji.

"Your goofy smile has only gotten bigger. Spill."

"All I told him was that me responding so quickly was on you."

Before I could put the phone down, it pinged with his response.

He sent back a grinning emoji.

*I was thinking... And you can totally say no. I'd love to see you again. Would you like to go out sometime?*

"I just asked him out."

She made a noise that sounded like something a grade schooler with a secret to tell might make. "You did not!"

"Stop." Nothing like embarrassment caused by a friend. My face was crazy hot. I turned the phone to her, hoping he wouldn't respond while she was looking.

Just as I turned it back, the three dots popped up.

*Your timing is amazing. I was thinking about asking you the same thing.*

My sharp intake of breath forced Tamara's gaze back on me from her tablet.

*Our captain's wife has an art gallery opening next week. Most of the team is coming along with wives, girlfriends, boyfriends, etc. Come with me? Dinner after maybe?*

I wasted no time with my response: *I'd love to. Send me the details and we'll make a plan.*

"Holy crap. I've got a date for next week." My heart

beat like a drum, and I hoped it wouldn't explode from excitement and nerves

Her mouth dropped open. "You know I'm gonna want all the details if this happens. I'm booking a breakfast meeting for the next day."

"We're going to an event I suspect all of his teammates will be at. I don't know what you think's going to happen."

My heart fluttered as I considered what *could* go on.

Did I even know how to make a move? Maybe he'd do it.

"Maybe I should connect you with Kyle's brother, Bobby, so you two can trade notes from the sidelines."

"Well if you don't want to give me the dirt, hook me up." She looked at her watch and started gathering up her trash and closing the cover on her tablet. "I gotta go take a call with Tokyo. See you bright and early for one last presentation rehearsal."

"I'll try not to change too much before I call it a night."

She glared at me as she walked to the door. "Don't you dare touch a thing." Her tone was all business.

I wouldn't do that to the team. But I might make some notes where I might say some different things along the way.

I opened the presentation, but Kyle was lodged in my thoughts.

It meant a lot that Kyle not only asked me out but decided to bring me to an event with his team. I hoped my nerves would behave so I wouldn't get too closed off or trip over my tongue. At least I had a few days to get used to the idea of this coming up and do my best to not get too freaked out.

# THIRTEEN

## KYLE

Austin lived in a nice building on the perimeter of downtown. I had certain preconceived notions about how tech tycoons lived. Austin broke that. It wasn't the newest building around to be sure. There were newer, taller buildings near the arena where the city had been trying to reinvigorate things. This building had a good, lived-in feeling while clearly being well maintained.

I pulled my SUV into the circular driveway and parked in a visitor space.

As soon as I walked in, a young man behind the lobby desk greeted me. "Mr. Pressgrove, hello. How can I help you this evening?" He gave a shaky, nervous smile as he straightened his tie.

I've played for the Arsenal for seven years, but it always threw me to be recognized away from the arena or events. Kennedy dealt with it often as the captain and the face of the team. And while I'm on the starting lineup most games, having people call me by name in random settings like this surprised me.

"Kyle is fine." I smiled, and his smile grew larger. "I'm here to see Austin Murray in seventeen twenty."

"Yes, sir. One moment. I'll buzz him."

As he made the call, I glanced around the lobby. The tasteful mid-century look didn't fit with the outside of the building, but I quite liked it. It all felt like a living room with even the reception desk fitting the esthetics. A wall full of books over a small fireplace took up one side and added to the feeling of being in someone's home.

"I'm sorry Mr.— Kyle. Mr. Murray didn't answer. I've been on duty about an hour, and I haven't seen him come in, and he usually stops to check for packages and laundry."

I sighed. Given the texts we'd traded yesterday and today, I didn't expect him to be late today since we'd decided I'd pick him up and that I wanted to make sure we were there for Adriana's welcoming remarks. According to my watch, he still had two minutes before he was officially tardy.

"Is it okay if I hang out of here and wait? I am a little early."

The guy gave me a single nod. "Of course. There's water and coffee there." He pointed to an area adjacent to the shelves. "You can help yourself."

I nodded back and decided to kill time by looking at the books. The selection was an eclectic mix of fiction, with books I recognized but also many that I did not. A small plaque indicated that residents could borrow books and add ones they wanted to get rid of. Very cool idea to have a lending library like this.

After I read a few spines, I checked my phone. And then repeated the cycle.

The last text message from Austin came in shortly before noon when we'd talked about where we might want to go for dinner. We'd narrowed it down to tapas or pizza.

I also had no missed calls.

Austin had planned to get here with enough time to change clothes too.

We had a little bit of time to spare in our schedule to arrive. I'd give him five minutes, and then I'd go solo.

I texted him. *Where are you? I'm in your lobby.*

Typing bubbles appeared immediately. *Kyle, so sorry. Last minute stuff popping up all over the place. I'm walking out. Be there in fifteen.*

That didn't seem realistic given traffic this time of day. I checked the time again. Traffic between here and the gallery wouldn't be too bad. I could let this go for a little bit.

*Fine.*

I scanned the shelves and even made notes on a couple books I wanted to read. One was about a romance between a prince from England and the son of the president of the United States. I loved a good romance. Who doesn't like a little happy? The other one was far darker about murders in a Missouri college town and two cops who had to figure out who done it.

Five minutes had passed, and I texted again. I wanted to make sure he'd actually walked out. *How's traffic? Are you gonna make it?*

I sat on one of the comfy couches and scrolled Instagram. I clicked the heart on several pictures of the team already at the gallery. David must be there because some of them were on the official team feed. Adriana planned to donate some of the evening's proceeds to the team foundation, so no surprise that David was on hand to document the event.

A text message dropped down from the top of the

screen. *Sorry. Sorry. Sorry. I'll meet you there. People keep pulling me aside. It's been that kind of day.*

I should've just gone when he wasn't here when I arrived.

*Do what you need to do. I'll see you later.*

Slightly passive-aggressive and nebulous on my part. Frankly, I didn't expect to see him tonight. I pocketed the phone and headed for the door.

"Not waiting for Mr. Murray? Do you have a message?"

I looked back at the guy who'd been nothing but polite and eager to help and swallowed my bubbling anger. "No, thanks. I've been texting with him so it's all good."

"Great. Have a good night."

"You too."

As soon as my phone connected to the car, a torrent of text messages arrived.

The robotic voice read, "I'll be there. I promise. As soon as I get out of here, I'll be there. I know this is important."

I imagined him talking quickly into his phone to get out the messages he thought I wanted to hear. If I wasn't an employee with critical information, I'd always be far down the list of his priorities. I don't know how he could justify that. My parents kept close track of the commitments they made to me and Bobby, to each other, to friends and colleagues. It wasn't that they weren't flexible, but there was a way to handle things going wrong.

Austin didn't seem to have those rules. Whoever or whatever had his attention in the moment ruled, no matter what else he'd promised to do.

Was it worth trying to build something with Austin when a big part of his personality was something I had such a hard time tolerating? Did I want to change myself?

More texts came in.

I ignored them.

I could dictate a reply, but I didn't have anything to say. We'd see if he showed up or not.

I wanted to be proven wrong.

As I'd hoped, traffic was manageable to the gallery. The place was packed. Thankfully, someone had the foresight to arrange valet parking so I didn't have to circle endlessly looking for a spot. I pulled up behind a car that was being tagged and hopped out, leaving the keys behind. One of the people from the stand came up quickly and gave me a claim ticket.

Inside, a lot of people were clustered in the front room. Beyond the large open area, people wandered through the smaller areas.

I waved at a group from the team as I shucked off my overcoat and handed it off to coat check. As soon as my hands were free, a waiter offered a wine and hot cider. Another perfect touch because the warm drink was exactly what I needed.

Adriana had created some amazing works. There were also some on display at Kennedy's house, but these were extraordinary. She'd created large-scale images of scenes from Detroit that mixed past and present. It fascinated me how she took something everyone knew and transformed it. From the downtown skyline to individual houses to some of the rundown areas of the city.

While talking with my teammates, I ended up looking beyond them to the art.

Talking to Crenshaw, I saw it.

I did my best to extract myself from the conversation without being rude before walking over to a wall that had two larger pictures but also several smaller ones. The one that drew my attention was of Joe Louis Arena. The image showed many decades: from before the arena existed to its construction on to its heyday and the more recent demolition.

My chest tightened and goose bumps crawled over my arms. I blinked back a tear. The picture was gorgeous and brought such a mix of happy and sad.

I reached out and stopped just short of touching it. The amount of texture and materials she used gave the image incredible motion—like a time lapse.

"You like it?"

I jerked, and the cider in my mug sloshed out onto my hand. I looked at Adriana, embarrassed.

"I'm so sorry. I didn't mean to startle." She put her hand on my forearm and smiled. I returned what had to have been the most sheepish grin ever.

"This is stunning." I struggled to find more to say, but I was afraid I'd sound lame.

"You've been standing here for quite a few minutes."

"I played my first pro game there. I played in our last game there." My words got caught on an unexpected lump in my throat. "My dad took me there when I was five to see the Arsenal."

I took a minute to compose myself, willing tears not to fall. Adriana simply stood there, and we looked at the picture together. This captured all of that and the before and after. To the right of the picture, a small card showed its name, "Remembering the Joe," and cost, thirty-seven hundred dollars.

"I remember seeing Terry in a game there shortly after we started dating. The incredible energy of the crowd was nothing like I'd ever experienced. I barely knew hockey, but I loved watching him skate. After so many years spent in that building, it was an obvious choice to create an image. I hope I did it justice for anyone who's been there."

"You have." Damn it. I had to wipe at my right eye.

Adriana hugged me across my shoulders. "It means a lot that it's moved you this way."

I looked at her, and we traded small smiles. "Who do I talk to about buying it? I would like to hang this in my house."

# FOURTEEN

## AUSTIN

KYLE HAD every right to be pissed. His message came through loud and clear in his text.

When it came to business, I was on time or gave a heads up that I'd be late and if the meeting could start without me.

While I should've extended the courtesy to Kyle that I did to my work colleagues, I probably should've begged off for the night because I still had things to review. Coming off last week's presentation, we had follow-ups due at the end of the week. Plus, Chevy came forward and said they wanted a review of our plans for the two years remaining on our contract, which didn't seem like good news.

My need to see Kyle and apologize overrode the urge to work.

As long as I had feedback to the team by morning, it'd be fine. Truth be told, I could probably take care of everything first thing, but as usual, I didn't want to be a holdup if anyone wanted to get started early.

Looking inside once I'd passed off the car to the valet, I took a deep, steadying breath. I didn't see Kyle but the place was packed. Crowds weren't my favorite, especially social ones. Managing strangers in a business setting came easily. When I had to interact with people I didn't know among a sea of others, it stressed me out. Words escaped me, I got jittery. I didn't like it, but I'd get through it like I had at the auction.

I turned on the charismatic, confident person I am for work gatherings. I'd be worn out later, but Kyle needed to know his importance to me.

Despite the chill, I stayed outside to scan the crowd. I hoped to spot Kyle so I could go directly to him but not all of the gallery was visible from the front windows.

I took out my phone and brought up his text screen. He hadn't even seen my last couple of texts. Was he ignoring me or simply not checking because he was busy in there?

The longer I stayed outside, the more my nervousness increased exponentially. So many butterflies swirled in my stomach, I considered leaving to make it stop.

I needed to take the leap and get in there, join the party, and take whatever lumps I had coming for being a late jerk.

Entering, I immediately warmed up and held back a sigh as the air felt good on my face. I still didn't see Kyle. He had to be here.

"Take your coat, sir?" asked one of the many people working the event. They were everywhere in black pants, white shirts, and black vests. Typical attire. This was a well-managed event.

"Yes, thank you." As I took it off and handed it over, I spotted a bluish gray peacoat that I'd seen Kyle wear on one of the racks. Fingers crossed that it was his.

With a glass of wine to settle my nerves, I moved into the crowd. It looked like the entire team was here, including coaches.

"Mr. Murray. I thought that was you." I turned and found David approaching. "You looking for Kyle?"

"Yes. Yes, I am."

"I saw him a couple minutes ago in the alcove over there." He pointed off to an area in the rear of the gallery. "I think he's found a picture he likes."

"Thanks."

He'd mentioned that he liked Adriana's work. It would be interesting to see exactly what he was in to. Disappointment crept over me because I missed that moment when he discovered the image that spoke to him. I liked moments when his eyes lit up in recognition of something—whether it was food he enjoyed, me skating better, or whatever. Tonight, I'd missed out because I didn't prioritize our date.

Kyle stood with the artist and another woman who was dressed in a very smart gray suit, perhaps the gallery owner. They were in the middle of the space, but I had a good guess about what he'd bought. The image of The Joe was amazing.

I stayed put for a moment and watched them talk.

Hesitation served no purpose. I took a breath and approached. I stepped in next to Kyle and offered a quick nod and a smile to him so I didn't interrupt Adriana.

He gave me a tight smile in return.


"IT WAS REALLY great to be able to get additional access because of Terry. I think the building manager thought I was crazy, scraping bits of paint and taking small bits of other materials from the interior and exterior. I also flew a drone before and during the deconstruction to get some of the images."

She looked to me as she finished her thought and then another look at Kyle.

"Adriana Kennedy and Sarah Katz, this is Austin Murray, my date." He explained that Sarah owned the gallery, and I extended my hand and greeted them.

I opted to save my apologies for when we were alone. "You're the proud owner of The Joe picture now?"

"Yeah. I am." His eyes were bright and excitement came into his voice, erasing the look he'd first given me. "What you heard was some of the material that she's put into it. I've now got a small piece of the arena forever."

"I'm so glad it resonated with you," Adriana said. "I'd hoped it would end up with one of you guys."

Sarah checked her watch. "We should have you make your remarks. It's about quarter till."

"Of course. Kyle, please excuse me. Austin, great to meet you."

"Mr. Pressgrove, I'll have your paperwork shortly. Thank you again so much."

Sarah and Adriana went toward the front of the gallery, and Kyle turned his attention back to his new purchase.

"This is really incredible. Come see."

Kyle brought me over and excitedly pointed out where there were actual materials, like the paint scrapes, being used as part of the layering Adriana had done. The excitement that rolled off him filled me with warmth, but it was tinged again with regret that I hadn't seen him discover the picture.

"Do you have anything else from the arena?"

"I've got my locker, which I have in my guest bedroom. If I ever build my own place, I'll figure out exactly the right use for it. The players got to take some stuff before they started marking things for the auction. I wish I'd taken more, but I tried to be realistic about what I might actually display because I didn't want to just put stuff in storage."

As attention was called to the front room, people moved in that direction, leaving us mostly alone.

I reached for Kyle's hand, and he let me take it. "I'm sorry." I spoke softly. "I know my track record with you sucks. All I can do is apologize and try to do better."

He nodded, his jaw tight. He held in what he truly wanted to say, probably due to the venue

I dropped my head, unable to hold his gaze. "I understand. I—"

"I'm trying to do better too." That spark in his eyes from when he showed me the picture was gone, and now he looked troubled. "I hold too much on things I was told as a kid. I need to be more understanding that things can come up." He sighed but some of the sadness lifted. "Let's go listen to Adriana. Then we'll enjoy the rest of the night and decide what's next."

I nodded but said nothing. We ended up smiling at each other, and he squeezed my hand. As we joined the crowd around Adriana, his confident smile returned, and I put on my best networking face.

I had hope. He hadn't broken it off. I had time to figure out how to be a good boyfriend.

# FIFTEEN

## KYLE

I'D HAVE to get off the ice soon because they'd open for seating. The PA played great pop tunes, and I'd gotten partially in gear to skate solo and center myself.

West Coast road stints were the worst. I'm okay with two or three days on the road, but after that, I had to fight against being cranky. I had distinct homebody tendencies.

The team started in Anaheim, where we'd lost in overtime, and we were in Vegas for an afternoon game that we expected to win. We'd stay here overnight and then hit San Jose before heading home.

I'd traded a few texts each day with Austin. He was traveling too—at a conference in Atlanta. We kept up with each other's day. His meetings frustrated him so he focused on trying to tell me something he enjoyed about the day and asking more about what travel was like for the team. I enjoyed hearing about his trip to the Coca-Cola Museum, which he retreated to after a grueling meeting day. He liked sampling the sodas from around the world, and I'd agreed that sounded cool.

I kept my cranky road persona from him—at least I think I did. Over the years, I'd learned how to focus on the game and not fixate on the million and one things that could happen with Mom and Bobby while I was on the opposite side of the country. I saw a therapist a couple of years ago, and I'd gotten some good tips on how to keep my shit together for these stretches. After all, the team didn't need to deal with my mood.

After the game, the team planned to find a good meal together—Vegas did have great food choices—and then split up. Those of us not into the gambling were looking for a concert or show to see. I'd put my suggestion in for any of the many Cirque du Soleil shows since I wouldn't mind seeing some hot, bendy guys on stage.

My pre-game skate reminded me of Austin and made me smile. We needed another day like that. Adriana's opening was tainted with his lateness, which we talked through at dinner. Before we'd hit the road and he'd come over for a Netflix and chill, which turned into a *Parks & Rec* marathon with chocolate and wine. I'd liked that a lot. It had been comfortable since we both loved the show, so we'd talked about favorite parts. It'd been perfect.

Whenever he avoided workaholic mode, Austin's charm came through, and he had so many of the qualities I wanted from a guy. Work though... If he lost himself there, it got difficult for me. I didn't want to totally piss him off, but I didn't know how much of that I could tolerate—or for that matter how much I should.

Of course this whole thing could be fleeting with the trade possibilities. I suppose it's flattering that another team wanted me, but I loathed the idea of a move. I hadn't heard anything new recently, and I was sure my agent was getting tired of me asking.

My current contract didn't include trade protection and I had another season to play before I'd negotiate again. I'd planned to request it. But right now, I had no influence and if a trade got brokered, I'd be gone in the blink of an eye.

I hoped that the good year I was having made me valuable enough to keep. On the other hand, it could make me attractive to other teams. Everything had a price, and if a team offered someone the Arsenal wanted—and word was we wanted defensemen—I didn't stand a chance.

The buzzer over the scoreboard sounded, and that was my signal to clear out. The Zamboni headed out onto the ice, and once the surface was ready, the team would hit the ice for regular warm-ups.

As I went to the locker room, David fell into step next to me. "Hey man, was about to come get you. You got a visitor. He knows you've only got a few minutes, but I told him I'd see if you could spare a couple."

A visitor? Here? That didn't happen often on the road, and I usually knew about it in advance.

"You guys must be having a helluva thing for Austin to show up here."

"Seriously?"

He nodded. "Yeah."

Well damn. "Can you please let Kennedy know where I am?"

"Sure thing."

Austin turned as I clomped into the room. It was impossible to walk in skates and not sound like Big Foot was coming. His smile lit up the room, and he looked amazing in dark jeans, a Detroit T-shirt, and a sport coat. My heart flipped in my chest and my road trip funk evaporated.

"Oh, great, David found you. I cut it close. That's the

problem trying to be spontaneous. I know you're here overnight, so I wanted to see if you're free after the game."

Austin came across the country for a date.

Impressive.

I grinned so big I thought my face might split.

"It's so good to see you." I stepped forward, and he pulled me into a tight hug. It felt weird with me taller than him because of the skates—usually he was a touch taller.

The embrace felt good, despite the gear that kept me from feeling too much of him.

"Oh good," he said, relief obvious. "I worried this might be a bad choice."

So freaking adorable. I'd never had a guy do something like this, and this gesture touched my very core, setting my heart aflutter. "What did you have in mind?"

"I was thinking... God, you may think this is super silly or weird or I don't know... A Cirque show?" He spoke quickly, but I heard every awesome word.

"No way! Seriously?" He looked stricken, misreading my excitement. "That's so cool. I was trying to get some of the guys to go to one tonight. I'd love to go—just us." This time I gave him a bear hug.

"Yo, KP. It's time," Kennedy called from down the corridor.

"I gotta..." I gestured at the door

"Go. I'll meet you back here after. What show should I get?"

"Your pick. Surprise me."

"You got it."

"Great." I headed for the door but turned back before I got into the hall. "It's really cool you're here."

I waved with my gloved hand, and he waved back, looking deliriously happy. I'm sure I looked the same.

I can't believe he did that.

Another proof that non-working Austin was a good guy. *Please don't let me get traded*, I silently prayed to the hockey gods. I wanted to see what this could be.

# SIXTEEN

## AUSTIN

After the amazing show—holy crap, those people were flexible—we walked on The Strip.

"Thank you for that. I loved it. I haven't been to a show in a long time." Kyle sounded so happy. Pride swelled in me since I'd been able to cap off his winning day with a show he'd enjoyed.

"Why don't you go to more?"

"This is lame. I honestly don't think to do it. I don't pay enough attention. Hell, Cirque comes to the arena, as do a lot of concerts. I usually find out about something once it's sold out."

"You couldn't pull strings to get a ticket?"

"I probably could, but I don't like doing that unless it's for someone else."

He gave so much. I'd seen that in just the short time I'd known him. He gave time to Hockey Allies and other charities. He gave time to his family. He worked with the team on community projects. Impressive didn't begin to cover it.

"You do better than me. I find out after the event's gone

and I end up reading about it or someone in the office saw it. The only thing I can keep up with is hockey."

"I used to go to concerts regularly during high school in the off-season. Bobby and I liked the same music and friends would come along too. We'd see which bands were coming and sort out what we could all afford."

"What was your favorite?" As I asked, he moved us toward the Bellagio where the fountain show was in progress.

"Has to be Beyoncé. Saw her when I was sixteen. We'd all obsessed over 'Single Ladies.' When it was announced she'd play Auburn Hills, we were all over that."

I remembered that song from the skating play list.

"What was your first?"

I shrugged "I didn't go to my first concert until I was in my junior year of college. I had a friend in the jazz band, and she convinced me to come to her show. It was good, although not really my kind of music. I'm more of a pop guy like you."

"Nice. Good to have similar music taste. Do you mind if we catch the next fountain show? It's one of my favorite things here."

I kept learning more about Kyle—small things, but so good to know. This trip was so the right thing to do.

"Sure. Lead on." He took my hand and navigated us through the people. He kept us close so we could talk.

"Any standouts since then?"

"No. I had it in my head not to spend money on that. You have no idea how much I overcame with myself to buy season hockey tickets once I had the money for it."

"We need to get you out more. It seems like there's events missing—skating, concerts..."

*We.* I liked the sound of that. Could that happen?

"I'd never really considered that my life was lacking. There had to be things you missed playing as much hockey as you did."

He stopped us as the crowd got denser closer to the fountains. "Of course. But I was playing the best game ever." As usual, when he talked about the game, he got animated. "The only thing I'd change was how much I fixated on being away from home. Travel has never been something I liked. Especially long trips like this one. I know deep down it's ridiculous, people travel all the time. I worry something will happen at home. I've got that under more control than when I was a teenager. I used to get so anxious..."

Kyle looked at the fountains as they continued dancing to the music.

"I'm being terrible." He turned his focus to me. "You told me about how you grew up, and I'm going on about the most ridiculous stuff. I'm sorry."

"It's okay. We've all got our own stuff. I honestly think my childhood was okay. I knew people who were hungry or didn't have adequate clothes. All in all, it could've been worse for me."

He hugged me close, putting his arm around my shoulders. The touch sent shivers through me—and not the cold kind. If anything, I warmed up by a few degrees. "Is there a big thing that you want to do and haven't?"

I instantly knew what the answer was, but could I share it? I didn't think he'd laugh. I took the leap. "I've always wanted to go on a vacation where I could let go, be myself, and be around a bunch of other gay guys—like Province-town during carnival or a gay cruise. I've never had the right people in my life to take that kind of trip with."

Admitting that felt good, but at the same time, embarrassment overtook me. It must sound so weird to him after growing up with a gay brother and having a friend like G.

I was in over my head, and yet I calmed as his shining eyes remained locked on me.

"That sounds fun. I've never done anything like that either. I've been to Detroit Pride many times, and there's an awesomeness about being inside a big crowd of people like you, and it's always better when I'm there with just the right people."

"Would it be crazy if... maybe... we went this summer?" Kyle's eyes went wide as I stammered out the question. "Only if we're still... you know... together and stuff. I get that when your summer starts varies on the playoffs and finals and there's a lot of time for me to mess this up..."

The crowd began to dissipate as the show ended. We stayed rooted in place, making the crowd go around us.

"I could just as easily mess us up," Kyle interjected. "You might get tired of me and my weird quirks around time, focus, and shit."

"The change that needs to happen."

The slightly furrowed brow that Kyle got when he thought appeared. I'd seen this a few times. At the same time that I found it sexy, I wanted to smooth it out. Tonight in particular, neither of us should be overthinking.

"Mom and Dad talked about punctuality all the time, and it's stuck with me. I remember I had a fit because I didn't want to go to somebody's house when I was four, maybe five. It was a playdate and time for Mom to have coffee and hang out with one of her friends." Kyle opened up more, and I took it all in eagerly. "When it became clear that we would be late, my mom called Miss Mary and I had to explain how sorry I was for making us late. After that, I was never one to be tardy to school and never was late to practice. If anything, I show up early. And anytime I'm going to be late, I get a message to whoever I'm meeting."

A new crowd formed since the next show would soon start.

"Come on, over here, my favorite place to watch." Kyle pointed to a light post.

He'd talked about that childhood moment so reverently —no wonder he gave me a hard time.

"We never had big lessons on manners." I picked up the sharing. "The expectation was that I would behave. I certainly made sure to be punctual with them, my jobs, with school. With all they had me doing, I didn't make close friends until college, and then they were all driven to succeed too. That's why I'm so close to Tamara; we very much had the same views. I know it sounds like my parents were horrible, but the lessons they gave me about living within means and getting into a good job propelled me to where I am today. Seems like your parents did pretty good by you too."

"For sure," Kyle said as we got to where he wanted to stand. "We were certainly middle class. I never had the sense that we lacked, but I lived in my own bubble too. Put me on the ice and I was happy. Bobby and I were always close since there was just a little over a year between us. Mom and Dad loved each other so much." His breath caught like he was reliving a memory. "If they had any issues, they didn't put them in front of us. All I remember with them is love. I can only imagine what they would've been like as I got older. Mom's great, but I think she still misses her other half."

"Is it terrible that I think my parents are still together because it's all that they really know? The past two or three years, even though I've made sure they're comfortable, I have a feeling that they think it's them against the world. I wish I could take that burden off them."

Kyle drew me close as he leaned against the pole, and I nestled into him.

"Parents." He raised his eyebrows. "Did they break us?" His tone was playful, but I wanted to be careful with my answer.

"Break us? Nah. Just need to modify some of the programming. What they taught us wasn't bad, it just needs to be applied differently."

Kyle grinned at me as the lights dimmed around the enormous fountain, signaling the show start. "I should've expected that kind of answer from a techie. I like it."

He held my gaze even as the show started. Anticipation burst from my chest.

Was he going to kiss me?

He squeezed my hand a couple of times and then jerked his toward the fountain. "Check it out. It's starting."

Probably for the best, but damn, a kiss would've been incredible. What would he taste like? How did he kiss?

I wanted to know.

# SEVENTEEN

## KYLE

WE ARRIVED back home with a road record of 1-1-1. That road performance exceeded our norm, and we wanted to bring that momentum into our next home game. We had a couple of days before that happened, so I settled back into the home routine.

The time with Austin in Vegas topped the highlight reel from the trip. After the fountain, we'd walked, occasionally wandered into hotels neither of us had been in to see if there was anything interesting, and, best of all, we'd talked a lot. We knew a ton more about each other, and I wanted to keep things going.

As I drove to Austin's office, hoping to steal him for the afternoon, the music I played cut out with a phone call. I grinned at the name on the display.

"G! Good to hear from you, man. Where are you today?"

"Hey, K. I'm home but headed out this afternoon. I can tell I got you in the car. This a good time?"

Wow. He sounded far more serious than usual. "Yeah.

Trying to hijack Austin to go teach hockey moves to some kids."

"Oh, nice. Another date so soon after his drop-in move. That's very cool."

"So, what's up? I can tell you've got something on your mind."

"Just wanted to see how you are doing."

"Okay, that's random."

"Oh man, you haven't seen it."

I gripped the steering wheel tighter, trying to steel myself for whatever he knew that I didn't. "Tell me. I'm sure whatever it is I'd rather hear about it from you."

"There's a story on the trade rumors site about what's expected within the next couple of weeks. And, well..."

Shit. The talk had seemed to die out recently, but that must've been the quiet before the storm.

"And they're right more often than not." I couldn't hold back a sigh as dread formed a big, throbbing ball in the pit of my stomach. "That sucks so hard. I'm glad you told me though. If it's out there, some of these kids may ask about it, and now I won't be blindsided."

"Have you talked to the coaches or management? Let them know you're really committed to staying in Detroit."

"My agent and I both have. And why the hell hasn't Candace called? It's her job to look out for stuff like this. Is it still sounding like Phoenix?"

"Yup. You and Helton to Phoenix in trade for Billington coming to Detroit."

Banging on the steering wheel did not quell my aggravation. After the coaching session, I'd have to talk to Candace to get more info.

"I have to ask, are you prepared to leave? You and Mamma P have talked, right?"

"Yeah." G and Bobby always checked on me with big stuff like this. "When I first found out the possibility, I let her know."

"And she was good?" G's voice betrayed that he knew the answer. Of course he did because he knew my family.

"Yeah." I chuckled, remembering the talk Mom, Bobby, and I had over Thanksgiving. "And of course she said it'd all be fine."

*You're the man in the house now* had echoed through my head during that conversation. I didn't know how to keep that up if I ended up across the country. Bobby and Sebastian weren't going to move to Detroit since their lives were in Chicago. Mom would have no family left here.

"You're overthinking this right now. I can practically hear your brain whirring." G never minced words. "Mamma P might kick my ass for telling you this, but she called me this morning to check on you because she saw the article. She's worried about how you'd react. You know she's surrounded by friends and loves her job. As far as I can see, she really loves her life."

Nervousness crashed through me, making me shake. I hated this discussion. Moving let the family down. It didn't matter that it had been nearly twenty years, people had told me I was in charge. Rationally, I knew I shouldn't hang onto those words. It was only something that a child got told, and it didn't mean a lifetime commitment.

Sometimes I was such a mess. Not completely unlike Austin and his fierce devotion to work. Maybe I needed to go back to the therapist for how to cope with this potential move.

"K? I lose you?"

"Sorry, I'm here. Just thinking how I need to stop being

the eight-year-old who needs to make sure Mom is okay every second of the day."

"There's a lot of people who'd be on it if either of them needed help and you weren't nearby."

I pulled up in the parking lot of Austin's office building and took one of the visitor spaces.

"I heard you pull the keys out so you've arrived and I should go. Call me if you need to talk, and keep me posted too, okay?"

"Thanks. Love ya, man. Talk later."

I disconnected and hopped out of the car. It'd gotten colder. There was talk of snow overnight, and as the sky took on a more slate look, I didn't doubt it.

Inside it only took me a moment to get past security and up to the second floor where Austin's office was.

"Kyle." A guy who looked about the same age as me—and Austin for that matter—looked up from his keyboard. "Hello. I'm Jack, Austin's assistant. Is he expecting you?"

I'd heard about Jack, the guy who apparently struggled to keep Austin on track, and I was about to derail that, at least for the afternoon.

"Hi, Jack. And, no. I'm trying to surprise him and hijack him for the afternoon. What's his schedule look like?"

"Lots of internal meetings." Jack looked disappointed. "He's booked until seven."

Extracting him from a schedule that lasted for six more hours did not seem possible.

"Can you show me those appointments, Jack?" A woman appeared next to me. She offered a smile before looking at Jack's screen. It only took her a moment before she faced me again "Good to meet you, Kyle. I'm Tamara."

"Yes. Austin's told me a lot about you. It's good to meet you."

"Let me see if I can pull him away for you. An afternoon out would do him some good." She scanned the screen and pointed at a couple entries. "Can you reschedule these to the morning? I can take the rest."

"Sure thing." Jack picked up his headset and started making calls.

"Go ahead and have a seat, Kyle, while I see what I can do. Do you have somewhere to be?"

Had Austin told her about my punctuality hang up?

"I need to be at the rink in forty-five minutes. If I leave here within twenty, it's good."

She nodded. "Got it."

Raised voices seeped out as she went in Austin's door. I suspected she had an uphill battle ahead. I shouldn't have done this, turning up at his work place. What was I thinking? It wasn't like showing up like he did in Vegas—that didn't have the complications. I just barreled in here. Probably not my best idea.

I pulled out my phone and surfed around, looking for news on the trade rumors. The article G mentioned had a lot of comments—all the usual type that ranged between displeasure and happiness. Most agreed that our defense needed help, which I couldn't disagree with. While we were winning recently, the teams we'd be up against in any playoffs were ones that our defense faltered against.

There was still a job for me to do for the team, so this couldn't fill my head. I'd hoped to make myself invaluable, but it suddenly felt like the point of no return had passed.

Austin's office opened, and he sounded extremely surprised.

"Are you seriously pushing me out the door?"

"Yes, I am." Tamara, on the other hand, seemed

amused. "You need to clear your head." She sounded quite stern.

"Oh, Kyle. Tamara neglected to say you were sitting right here." Austin put his messenger bag in the chair next to me and put his coat on.

"You two go have fun."

I stood, and she gently pushed Austin in front of me. A smile lit up his face, and it extended up to his eyes. It was gorgeous. A little heat rose in my cheeks at the power of that smile directed at me.

"I'm coaching some of the kids in an after-school program that you help support. I thought you'd like to come along."

We walked out of his office, heading for the stairs down to the lobby. "That sounds awesome. I've wanted to see the foundation at work. But middle of the day..."

I nodded. Missing part of a work day can be tough for parents, and it's one of the reasons why the after-school programs were so important. It gave kids a place to go. "Today it's important because one of the volunteers is home sick, so you're going to be working—just not here."

"Oh God, not on the ice I hope." He stepped back with terror in his eyes.

"I wouldn't do that to you. There's plenty to do off-ice." I gently took his forearm to keep him moving forward.

"What are you up to after?" The momentary tension drained from Austin as we walked. "I've been told in no uncertain terms that I'm not allowed back here for the rest of the day, even though it's a bonkers day."

I studied him and worried I'd gone too far. "If it's really not a good time, we can raincheck on this." I meant it, and I hoped I conveyed that.

He thought, but he also kept walking. "No. It's good. It

might be good to focus on something else for a while and let other parts of my brain work on the problems."

"Alright then. One afternoon of fun coming up. And to answer your question, I've got nothing planned after this until practice in the morning. Did you have anything in mind?"

"I have no doubt we can figure out something."

Score! I had an afternoon with Austin and he seemed happy to get away. I hoped this was good for both of us.

# EIGHTEEN

## AUSTIN

I MIGHT AS WELL HAVE BEEN in an alternate universe. Picked up and whisked away on a midday outing. That had never happened.

The choice of outing was excellent. Like I told him, I'd always wanted to do something like this. Kyle definitely pushed me out of my routine in great ways.

"What's the plan with the kids?"

"We've got young people from three community centers coming by to try out donated gear. If they like it, they get to keep it. They get to try out the gear on ice, skate around, and shoot a little if they want. I'll be out there coaching. One of the local rinks is also going to sign up students for a discounted hockey class, which your foundation also underwrites."

"Do you do this sort of thing a lot?"

He nodded. "As often as I can. Sports was so good to me I like to help others find that for themselves."

We pulled up in the arena parking lot by the player entrance. A cluster of vans was nearby and that must mean at least some of the kids were here. "That's why I started the foundation. I wanted to help get kids into whatever after school thing they wanted to do without worrying about paying for it. Give kids what I didn't have myself."

"I want to start something like that one day. I'm trying to, you know, structure my finances smartly while I'm earning this good money. I already make ridiculous amounts of money, and I need to make it work for me, my family, and the community."

"Another way we're sort of alike," I said as we got out of the SUV. "We want to make sure we don't lose our money."

"You might be right." He smirked at me.

We walked inside, and there were a few people around, some were players I recognized.

We headed into the locker room where a couple people put away things. It looked like laundry, maybe from the morning practice. Kyle said hello to the guys.

"I gotta lace up so I can be on the ice. Won't take a minute."

He seemed faster at getting in the skates than he had when we skated together. He was already in sweatpants, but after he hung his coat in the locker, he slipped out of the sweater he wore.

I restrained an audible gasp at seeing him shirtless for the first time. He had a perfect six pack and my mouth watered, wanting to lick around those ridges. A smattering of hair spread across his chest and a thin trail disappeared into his sweats.

I should look away.

He made no move to hide himself as he pulled a workout shirt over his head and then pulled on a Detroit jacket.

The image of his sculpted chest and abs was burned into my brain. I couldn't fixate on it now because I couldn't get aroused in these pants. Khakis didn't hide much, and we'd soon be around kids.

"And in case you hadn't heard," he said as we went to the ice, "trade rumors spiked today."

"Oh no. I hadn't seen that."

"Not a done deal, but it sounds far closer to it than I'd like." Kyle struggled to keep his mood up. "I just wanted to mention it in case you hear any chatter here."

I liked having the heads up but wished we could talk about it more. It'd be conversation for later.

The kids were closer to teens, most were between twelve and sixteen. I helped distribute gear and made sure the fit seemed right before they went on the ice. Sometimes they came back if something didn't feel quite right. I loved how much equipment was here—a mix of donated and new.

Kyle had a blast on the ice alongside one of his teammates. Once Kyle retired from play, I easily imagined him coaching. He had such patience. He'd shown that with my lesson but it was even more on display here. He stayed on the ice until the last of his students was called off.

The ninety minutes flew by.

When he changed after the session, I busied myself on my phone so I wouldn't stare.

"Everything okay at the office?"

"Seems okay." I scanned the subject lines and nothing stood out as urgent. If something was on fire, they'd mark it urgent or call and nothing had come in while we were on the ice when I had my phone off.

"If you need to go back, you can say so. I heard some of the raised voices earlier."

Ouch. He'd heard that. I'd been on the verge of losing my temper as one of our business development guys expressed a differing opinion on how we were handling follow up to the big presentation from last week. "Sorry you had to hear that. Things are more tense than usual with a couple clients in the balance and our yearly innovation summit coming up."

He put a hand on my forearm and the understanding look in his eyes warmed me. "Only if you're sure. I don't want you in trouble with your staff, or with yourself, because I stole you away."

"I'll have time later tonight or tomorrow to go over what's getting done." No way was I giving up this afternoon with him. Plus Tamara knows I'll pick up if she calls, and even though things are unsettled, she's someone I can count on."

"Do you want to pick up your car on the way to my place? Or, do you want me to drive you back after?"

His place. Interesting.

"I can get it later. I don't want to risk getting sucked into something. You can drive or I can call a car."

He nodded. "Off we go then."

He offered me a hand up from the bench, but he didn't let go afterward. Instead he held it as we left. Just as he started the car, his phone rang. On the dashboard, the word "Mom" appeared.

"Sorry."

I stopped him before he could tap "Ignore." "Don't do that. It's your mom. Take the call. I swear I won't hold it against you."

He studied me for a moment and smiled as he hit "Accept."

"Hi, Mom. I'm in the car with a friend. What's up?"

I liked how he immediately said that someone was with him. I imagined that was to keep the conversation away from anything that might be too personal, or maybe embarrassing.

"Oh. I didn't mean to interrupt. Voicemail would've been fine."

"I was about to send it there, but I was told not to." He winked at me. Too cute.

"Well, I'll only be a minute. I had a craving for lasagna, and since I had the time, I made it. I made a pan for you too. I can put it in my freezer, and you can get it later, or today. Whatever you want."

The noise of delight Kyle made was music to my ears. What else got him to do that? "You know that's my favorite. Can I just come get it now?"

"Of course."

He looked at me. I had no problem eating lasagna. And I imagined home cooking from his mom—who he already said could be a chef—would be pretty incredible. I lived a life of takeout because I didn't know how to cook. It'd be a treat no matter where we ate it. I nodded to indicate my okay to go get it.

"One second." He hit the mute button. "Are we to the point where we see parents?"

"I'm okay with it if you are."

"Okay then." He unmuted the call. "We're at the arena, so we should be there in about fifteen minutes. It'll make a good dinner."

"Perfect. I'll leave it in the oven on warm. See you soon."

He disconnected the call and music kicked on—the nineties channel from satellite radio.

If he was the least bit nervous about bringing me home, he hid it well as he asked, "So, lasagna for dinner?"

"Sure." The afternoon kept getting better. Not just dinner now, but his mom's cooking.

"I promise you've never had anything this good. Ever. And it beats anything we might've ordered in from my place. We can certainly binge some more *Parks and Rec*."

"I'd like that." It seemed the perfect continuation of the day. "Anything I should know about your mom? Topics to stay away from? Stories I should ask about you?" I grinned, which he caught. I got a brief evil glare in return.

"Don't you dare try to get stories on your first visit."

"No promises." I broke into a laugh. I'd managed to rile him a bit, which did not happen often.

"You're the most different guy I've ever brought home because you're not an athlete. She's good though, very relaxed. She'll ask questions in a way that you don't feel like you're being interrogated."

"Exactly how many guys have you brought home?"

"I guess I did make it sound like a lot." He hesitated. "I dated two guys in high school—one between sophomore and junior year and another most of my senior year. And I dated a football player part of my freshmen college year. Once I got drafted, it's really only been occasional hookups. So you're the third I've brought home—the football player didn't make it that far."

No one in the seven years since he joined the Arsenal. I envied him having high school boyfriends. I remembered him being out back then, but I didn't recall any dating gossip about him—then or now. Although I wasn't exactly plugged in either.

"I've never brought anyone home. No one's ever been serious enough."

"Maybe you'll change that soon." The earnestness in his

voice nearly cracked my heart open. Did he want to turn us into boyfriends? Could I be one that he deserved?

He turned onto a street lined with houses. They were well-kept and some appeared to be recently renovated.

"This the neighborhood you grew up in?"

"Yeah. It was a great neighborhood. A lot of people left when the city got depressed, but some of Mom's best friends are still here, and the new families who have moved in are good people."

"I have these visions of you playing street hockey out here."

He pulled into a driveway. The garage door was open with an SUV identical to his—except it was red and his was black—parked inside.

"You'd think, but no. We were snobs and our hockey had to be on ice. There was a kid who lived down the street and his dad froze a small rink in their backyard for winter. The ice was pretty terrible but we made do, and you couldn't beat a sheet of ice right here."

We got out and met at the front of the car.

"You ready for this?"

I nodded, and we traded grins.

I followed him to the door that led into the house from the garage. He looked behind and gave me one last grin before he opened the door.

"Hey, Mom," he said as we entered. The aroma of the lasagna hit me immediately and my mouth started to water. Signs of the day's cooking showed with a stack of pans in the sink and splatters of sauce on the stove top. She stood at the sink working on the stack.

"Kyle. Hello. I'd say sorry about the mess, but I'm not because it was worth it." She grinned as she dried her hands. I saw aspects of Kyle in her face, especially her nose,

121

mouth, and cheeks as well as the dark hair. She came over and hugged Kyle followed by a quick kiss on his cheek. "And you must be Austin. Good to meet you. I am a hugger. Is that okay?"

She waited a beat, and I appreciated that I had the opportunity to decline but no way I'd refuse a hug from this vibrant person. I opened my arms, and we had a brief, warm hug. Happiness rolled over me. I'd only been here a minute but I knew this house radiated love and contentment. That feeling started with her and had to be where Kyle got it.

"Good to meet you as well, Mrs. Pressgrove."

She waved her hand in front of her. "None of that. You can either call me Greta or Mamma P like Kyle's bestie Garrett does."

I gave a nod. "Okay, Greta it is." It didn't feel right going right to the name Garrett used while Kyle and I were still early in our relationship. It'd be awesome to use it one day though.

"What are you two up to tonight?"

"Well, first thing is going to be some amazing lasagna— I've talked it up on the way here—and then probably chill with something on TV."

"It's hard to beat quiet nights like that."

"Since you're feeding us, why don't we finish the cleanup?" I hoped Kyle wouldn't mind that I took the liberty on that, but it seemed the least we could do.

"Great idea." He took off his coat, and I did the same. He hung them on hooks by the door while I pushed up my sleeves and headed to the sink.

"Oh. I like this one." She touched my forearm and smiled as I passed. He didn't seem to mind the remark, and I certainly didn't. I got the Mom Thumbs Up.

Kyle washed and I dried. We put dishes away as we

went, with his mom sitting at the island directing me where to put things. In between, we talked about the hockey season and even about the possible trade.

"You seem awfully calm about all this," Greta said with a bit of a mom tone.

"I don't want to go, but unless I'm going to quit, there's not much I can do."

"I'd prepared for a tantrum." I caught the slightly evil glint in her eye as I went from cupboard back to the sink.

"Seriously, Mom?" Kyle whirled around from the sink, sponge dripping on the floor. The mortified look on his face was priceless—you'd think she'd brought out baby pictures. "You say that in front of the first guy I've brought home in ages."

My heart leapt once again to be referred to that way. He hadn't said boyfriend, but it hovered so near that designation.

"If he doesn't know already, he should know the moods you have." They exchanged smirks. "Anyway, I'm glad you're doing okay."

She pivoted to the safer topic of what I did for work.

I loved meeting his Mom. He'd been right, very low stress—even as she picked on him a bit. As we left, I really wanted to get to the point that I could call her Mamma P.

# NINETEEN

## KYLE

"Should I have called you boyfriend earlier?" I dropped the question while I served up the lasagna. Austin assembled small salads since I had some makings in the fridge, and I probably just made the whole thing awkward. "I wasn't sure. We were talking about guys I'd brought home and that usually means boyfriend but—"

"It was fine." He looked at me, pausing his dicing. I quietly let out a breath of relief. "You could if you wanted to though."

I reached out for his hand, taking it in mine. He squeezed once and my insides got all fluttery at the show of affection. The fluttering happened a lot lately, sometimes just thinking about him could induce the feeling.

"We could make it official?" I got my phone off the counter. "It can be a twofer—I can call you my boyfriend, and Bobby can be jealous I've got lasagna and he doesn't."

"An announcement with a side of brotherly harassment. I like it."

We positioned ourselves so we were close. I held the phone out while Austin held up a plate of food. Once we settled on the perfect look, we smiled and I snapped the picture.

He looked brilliant—bright eyes, sweet smile. We appeared much more relaxed than we had at the auction.

I showed him the pic.

"Damn. We're a good-looking couple."

We burst out laughing.

"We are kind of cute," I said once we settled down. "Do you want me to tag you?"

"Go for it, and then I'll repost too. Might as well do it at the same time."

I typed, the right words coming easily. *Austin and me about to eat Mom's famous lasagna. That's right, Bobby, I got a pan of lasagna and you didn't. Tell Seb I'm sorry you guys aren't eating as well as we are. #bejealousbrother #mealwith- theboyfriend #momhomecooking*

I tagged Austin in the photo. I didn't tag Bobby or Seb. I wanted them to stumble onto it because it'd be all the sweeter.

"Alright. It's out there. I'll bring the food to the couch while you do the repost."

He started on his post as I carried plates. Meeting Mom and announcing on Insta. That was a double whammy. I hoped it wasn't too fast. Or that I'd made a bad choice. I liked him so much. Still, many things could go wrong. For now, I wanted to enjoy it though.

He turned his phone to me when I got back. *Got to meet the boyfriend's mom today. She gifted him with homemade food. It's a great date night. #meettheparents #mealwiththe- boyfriend #momhomecooking*

"Nice."

"I borrowed a couple hashtags. I hope that's okay."

"Of course."

He put his phone next to mine on the counter. My only reaction, which I wasn't sure he saw, was to smile. I grabbed a couple beers from the fridge, and we padded into the living room. We'd both ditched out shoes when we'd gotten here, and Austin had hung up his sport coat along with his overcoat.

"Cheers. Thanks for a wonderful day." Austin held out his bottle and I clanked mine against it.

"You're welcome. It's been great."

We drank and then attacked the food.

"My God," Austin said, "you didn't do this justice. It's incredible."

He immediately took another bite.

"It's difficult to savor. I have to pace myself because it's so yummy I just want to devour it."

With the good food, talking took a back seat. I enjoyed stealing glances as Austin ate. I swear, even though I'd picked him up hours ago, he continued to relax more. It made me comfortable that he was so comfortable, neither of us tiptoeing around each other. At least the immediate aftermath of labeling our relationship wasn't regret.

After two helpings, which was about half the tray, we called dinner done. As we put things away and cleaned up the kitchen, my phone vibrated with a text from G.

"This is either going to be congrats or giving me hell." I held the phone between us so we could read.

*Congrats. Loved that post so much. And it's not nice to taunt Bobby like that.*

I sent back a heart emoji and one with its tongue stuck out. I tapped over to check Insta.

Austin checked his too. "Wow. So many likes and nice messages."

"Me too, from teammates, fans, and Mom, although she also told me not to harass Bobby. He's yet to weight in."

I expected at least a few angry remarks. I wasn't the only one with a boyfriend on the team, but every time Greg posted pics with his man, he heard from a few haters. He ignored and block those people—no muss no fuss—and I'd follow his example.

Simultaneously, we checked the side switch to make sure the phones were silent before we put them back on the counter face down. Without a word, we headed back to the couch, as if we had a routine.

I liked it. I wanted it. Could I keep it though?

We settled on the couch—me in the corner and Austin next to me. Our legs touched. I leaned forward to grab the remote, but as I sat back, he took it from me. I shot him a questioning look.

"There's something..."

Had I done something wrong? Crap. The look on his face said he had something urgent. What changed from when we were in the kitchen?

"I've got no idea what I'm doing." Austin pivoted so one leg was folded on the couch and he could look directly at me. "I'd—"

I moved quickly so I wouldn't overthink. Drawing close to him, I crashed my lips into his. Instincts told me he wanted it, and my God, yes, I wanted it. For a moment, he seemed stunned but then he kissed back. The remote thudded as it hit the floor when he dropped it.

I pulled back just enough to look at him. The loopy grin told me I'd made the right choice.

"Yes. That. That's what I wanted."

We leaned into each other and touched foreheads.

"I'm glad I picked right. You had me worried for a minute."

Austin put his hand on my shoulder and he quaked. I took his other hand in mine.

"I would tell you not to be nervous, but I am too." I guided the shaking hand I had and placed it over my heart. "Feel it? It's about to pound out of my chest. Reminds me of how it thumps when I do suicide sprints."

Austin's shudders lessened. He planted the softest kiss on my lips, just barely pressing them together.

So gentle. So caring.

A shiver shot through me. He had to have felt that. My excitement hit an embarrassing peak. Austin responded by kissing me more. I moved my lips against his, matching his gentleness.

After a moment, I upped the intensity, running my tongue along his lips, which he parted ever so slightly to nibble at my tongue. Pleasure pulsed through me, exceeding anything I'd experienced with anyone else.

Sure, I was horny. It'd been months since I'd had anything other than porn and my hand. This was far more. The feeling of desire and that this was right had built in strength since Vegas. It showed no signs of stopping. Was this what Bobby and Seb felt?

I hesitated to take charge. Austin needed to be comfortable and enjoy this as much as I did.

"I know how jittery you are." Talking was the best way to sort it out, even though it might kill the mood. "We can pause, stop, whenever you need to."

"I feel like a freaking teenager." I liked that Austin sounded more amused than upset.

"It's okay. Believe me, there's a fleet of butterflies flying around inside me right now. Let's just see where this goes."

No date ever felt as romantic as this one did, and we hadn't even called this a date—but maybe it was.

When Austin had shown up in Vegas, I'd gotten all swoony. Since that night, we could've become characters in one of the romances I read sometimes.

I couldn't believe we were making out on my couch.

Austin's teenager remark was so much the opposite of his confident business persona. I'd seen him withdraw sometimes in crowds, like how skittish he'd sometimes gotten during the gallery opening.

Slow proved to be good for us though. I'd never spent so much time kissing—usually there was a hurry to get off. I didn't feel that, and I don't think he did either.

I pulled him gently toward me, and I adjusted so I leaned back and he could press into me. We never broke the kissing—he instinctively knew where he needed to go. He even rose up a bit so I could get my legs under him. I lay on the couch and he stretched over top of me.

He took more control, exploring my mouth and moaning with each breath. The noises spurred me on. He eagerly sucked my tongue while I ran my hands over his back. I untucked his dress shirt so I could touch his skin, which yielded more enthusiastic groans.

As he writhed on top of my pinned body, my cock throbbed. I still wore sweats and the tent would be obvious. Could he feel the hardness?

How far did he want to take this? Every kiss made me want to strip both of us. Stealing a look, I found his eyes closed. He seemed lost in the pleasure. This would be so much better if we had room to move.

I pushed him ever so gently.

"Everything okay?" Concern filled his voice while his eyes were a little glazed over; pleasure had done the same to me, I was sure. I'd never felt so wanted. He looked like he'd devour me if I let him.

"Oh yeah. I thought we could move to the bedroom so we could get more comfortable."

He nodded and stood, offering me a hand up.

A hiss of pleasure escaped me as Austin brazenly cupped my cock and balls gently once I was next to him. The provocative move was out of character and damn sexy.

"Damn. That's a helluva bulge."

I returned the gesture. His cock couldn't hide from my deliberate touch. "You're packing something pretty sizeable yourself." I grabbed his hand and navigated us around the coffee table. "Come on. Computer, turn on the light."

A soft tone sounded as the bedside table added some soft light to the room.

"Oh my God, that was totally geeky. You renamed your voice assistant for *Star Trek.*"

"I did." I proudly let my Trekkie flag fly. "Why call it some made up name when I can do something I've wanted to do since I was a kid? I was a *Next Gen, DS9, Voyager* fanatic in middle school and high school. I ate those re-runs up. It's still one of my favorite things to have on in the background."

I pulled off my sweatshirt, and I thought Austin might start to pant. He ran his tongue over his lips. I tossed the shirt on the bench at the end of the bed.

"I've wanted to see this again so bad. I didn't think it'd happen so soon." He ran a hand though his hair, ruffling it in a totally cute way. "You look amazing."

I fought the urge to shrug since I should just accept the compliment. I looked okay—a regular fit guy. "Again?"

"Yeah." He nodded. "You changed shirts in the locker room today."

I hadn't even registered that. The locker room to me is all business. At least he liked what he saw.

He came forward and ran his hand over my chest. I shuddered to my very core.

"Should I lose these too?" I put my hands on the waistband of the sweats.

Austin nodded quickly. "Please." His voice broke. The slight squeak proved sexier than the moans, making my cock ache to be free.

I lost the sweats and briefs at the same time, letting them stay on the floor. I stepped out of them and closed more of the space between us. He stared at my cock sticking straight out.

"Oh wow," he said softly.

# TWENTY

## AUSTIN

WE STARED AT EACH OTHER, the soft lighting playing off Kyle's eyes and casting shadows over parts of his amazing body. I'd dreamed about what he might look like, but the real thing far exceeded anything I'd come up with. His expression of desire had me frozen in place. I wanted to touch, but I didn't quite know how to proceed.

Kyle let me take my time. Stripping seemed a good way forward, but a kind of scary one too. I didn't have his build. Hell, I didn't have his anything. I didn't work out much either—mostly because I forgot to—so I was only saved by the fact I didn't eat a lot—again because I'd forget to.

Unbuttoning my shirt was a good start. I wished I hadn't worn a t-shirt under it because it was just one more layer I had to deal with. The most terrifying one too since my chest and abs couldn't compete with Kyle's.

He never moved his hungry gaze off me.

My shoes didn't behave. I couldn't get them toed off.

Damnit.

Now I looked like a klutz.

I grabbed at the shoes and pulled them off, looking a bit

like a spazzy flamingo while I did it. I kept the socks on to match Kyle.

Down to just jeans and boxers, I stopped short of popping the button.

"If this is too fast or too much, we can stop," Kyle said in a soft voice.

So sweet. He's clearly ready—that thick cock sticking out in front—yet he allowed me to go at my own pace.

"No. I want to. Just stupid flashbacks in my head. The jock and the nerd. My high school self is saying this can't end well."

Kyle stepped forwarded. "Let me show you how nice some jocks can be."

He dropped to his knees in front of me, moved my hands aside, and opened my jeans, kissing along my waist as he did it. The only response I had was to hum.

After a moment, I allowed myself to run my hands through his hair, which was so soft.

"You're one of the sexiest nerds I've ever seen." He looked up and held my attention as he slipped my pants down. The gentleness was an extension of this kindness I always witnessed from him—except of course for his ferocity on the ice.

With my dick free, he teased along the shaft with the tip of his tongue. My body threatened to vibrate apart. So much pleasure from the slightest touch.

"Hmmm. I think you liked that." He repeated the move in the opposite direction. "Yup. You definitely did."

"Please come up here and kiss me." I never sounded like that—a whispered growl. He had me so blissed out, it affected every part of me.

Despite the sensations Kyle provided, I needed his mouth on mine. I pulled on his shoulders and he relented.

I wrapped us in a hug and hungrily kissed him. Kyle seemed okay with me setting the pace, so I tamped the nervousness down and went for it. Pressed close, our cocks slid together and the electrifying jolts resulted in stars flashing before my eyes.

Kyle's tight body moved under my hands as he explored me. Every place we touched, sparked, pinpoints of pleasure popping along the surface.

As much I loved his mouth on mine, I was ready to taste more of him. I disengaged carefully from the kiss and lowered myself, running my lips down his chin, neck, and to his chest. I darted over to suck on a nipple and got the reward of a full body shiver.

I noted that for future reference.

After spending a few moments nibbling and sucking his nip, I continued down until his cock stood before me. Fighting against my overall nervousness, I ran my tongue over his rigid shaft. That got the loudest moan so far, and I hoped Kyle's neighbors couldn't hear. The moan was also a good "fuck off" to that niggling worry that I didn't know what I was doing.

I wanted so much more of Kyle—more in ways I couldn't even define. He had a fire in his eyes when I looked at him. He watched me taste all of him and that fueled me on.

Did I love this guy? Maybe. Nothing else had ever inspired me to try and change up my habits.

"Can I..."

I didn't stop my oral exploration of his cock and balls even as he tried to speak.

"I... Give me..."

Kyle Pressgrove had been rendered speechless by me. An inexperienced tech geek.

He ran his hand through my hair, mirroring what I'd done to him, before nudging me off his cock.

"Awwww." I looked up with a sad face.

"Austin." His breaths were ragged. "I need your dick." I sucked for a brief moment on the head of his. "Please." He stretched that word out, though I made his voice crack when I licked one of his balls. "Come on. No fair."

"Totally fair." Where had this take-charge guy emerged from? This unknown side of me needed to show up more often away from the office—able to be playful, taking what I wanted, and not freaking out. "I'm busy here."

"I want to be busy too. You're making me feel insanely good, and I want to get in on the fun. Your—" I sucked him all the way down, and he swallowed some words. "Your cock needs me," he said when I released him.

"If you put it that way, I suppose I can't really deny you."

I stood and admired his body all over again. His eyes heated me—not in an embarrassed way. Not at all. Feeling wanted by him seared my very soul.

Kyle stole some kisses before laying us down on the bed. He positioned himself so we could work on each other.

I returned to my exploring. My lips appreciated the textures of the skin pulled tight on his hard shaft. When I hit a sensitive spot that made him throb, I noted it on the mental map I was making of Kyle's body.

Touching his balls in any way got an immediate reaction. He moaned, which sent intense vibrations up my shaft.

How crazy could I make him? Caressing his flesh gently, moving the fine hairs over his skin, and getting my lips and tongue in on the action only made me hornier. My cock pulsed in his mouth, and every time it did, he sucked me to the very back of his throat. I fought to keep his cock in my mouth rather than allow it to slip out.

Teasing Kyle's balls really got his attention—the more I did it, the more he shuddered. His breaths came in shorter bursts. Could I get him to come while only doing this?

Running two fingers over his ballsac made his cock jump. I added my tongue to the mix and it pulled his focus away from my cock. He stopped sucking, but kept it in his mouth and moaned—the vibrations making incredible sensations against me.

Meanwhile, he shuddered more as I kept changing up how I touched him.

If I could get him to come, I wanted to swallow it down. While my hands kept up the sensations on his balls, I swallowed down his cock.

His whole body convulsed, and he let my cock go with a loud moan. "Oh, fuck, Austin... Jesus... So... good... fuck."

I chanced that I could suck him still deeper. Slow and steady I went. He shuddered and moaned and that only spurred me on as he ran his hand over my thigh.

I didn't care that he forgot about my cock. Having him like this was everything. His cock head hit the back of my throat, and I managed to handle it. While my tongue worked his shaft, his balls still had my attention. I kept one finger caressing because he'd made it clear with his noises that was a hot button.

One of his hands slammed into the bed as he called out. "Austin, I'm not gonna be able to hold back." He barely choked out the words.

I acknowledged only with my mouth and hand increasing the intensity.

He became a nonstop moaning machine—gasps, whimpers, growls, sighs, and sounds I didn't know how to name.

"Oh... that's it.... Last warning. Can't. Hold. It."

I stayed on his cock. I'd worked for this load, and I wanted to take all of it that I could.

Under my touch, his balls contracted and cock pulsed as he shot down my throat.

Fuck. He unleashed a torrent. Somehow, I took all of the salty sweetness without choking or losing too much of it.

Kyle's bucked under me, and he slapped the mattress a couple more times.

I held him in my mouth until he released a sigh of satiation. I slowly released his dick and licked up the few remaining drops.

"I thought you might suck my very soul out." Kyle's voice had a sleepy, dreamlike tone as he rolled onto his back. "Holy crap, that was amazing. How did you even..."

"You pointed the way. Once I figured out how sensitive your balls were, I just kept going."

I crawled up Kyle, feeling emboldened by how much he'd enjoyed what I'd done. He'd gotten me close before I distracted him, and my hard-on wouldn't be ignored.

"What are you up to?"

"Just sit back and enjoy the show." Internally, I flinched at how ridiculous that sounded. Did I even know how to put on a show? But I had to get myself off and enjoy more of Kyle while I did.

I positioned myself in a way that I could put his still semi-hard cock in my ass crack. We weren't going to fuck, it wasn't the right time for that, but feeling him against my ass would spur me on to finish.

I let out a long moan as he electrified all the nerves outside my hole. Kyle's eyes, already glazed, went wide as I sent more zings down his cock. He fisted the sheets and softly sighed.

A little bit of gyration kept up the sensations as I pulled on my steely shaft.

His gaze darted between my face and my hand, a sexy smile crossing his lips. I jerked hard and fast, and in no time, an orgasm triggered deep in my balls, and its power spread through me.

"Gonna come," I managed to say between gasps.

I shuddered so hard I almost fell off. Kyle's quick reflexes steadied me as he put his hands on my hips to hold me in place

The first two shots hit him on the cheek.

"Hell yeah." He sounded impressed.

So much cum unloaded, spraying his chest and stomach. I didn't know I had all that. When it stopped, Kyle released me, and I flopped over to lay next to him.

"Holy shit."

"Right?" He looked at me, and we held each other's gaze for a moment before we cracked up. "Fucking incredible."

We caressed each other for a few moments before I broke the quiet. "I feel like we need to clean up before this becomes a super sticky mess, but I don't know if I can move."

"Me either. Damn, that was amazing." He rolled back on his side and kissed me before continuing. "Declaring ourselves boyfriends and some mind-blowing sex all in one day. You doing okay with that?"

"We definitely unlocked a few achievements tonight, don't you think?" God, sometimes my geek flag flew too proudly.

"That would be a way to look at it." He didn't make fun, instead he gently kissed me more. I doubted I'd ever get tired of that. "Let's hit the shower before we get too sleepy. You maybe want to stay here tonight?"

Did I? I hadn't thought about that yet. "I'd like that." I didn't want to give myself a chance to second guess it.

Tonight, I'd sleep next to this incredibly hunky man who I didn't want to let out of my life. He'd certainly be worth creating a work-life balance for. And if the trade happened, we'd figure it out. People move for jobs all the time.

# TWENTY-ONE

## KYLE

"So you've officially got a boyfriend now? We can stop dancing around who Austin is to you?" Bobby, of course, boiled it all down.

"Can it get any more official these days than a post like that?"

"It certainly drew my attention away from the fact Mom made you guys lasagna. I think it took like six months before Seb got one of those."

"Ha!" I might have shouted too loudly into the phone. "It only took that long because it took you that long to bring him up here."

"Point taken. Next time you're in Chicago, I expect you to bring him so I can get to know him better. I had no idea you'd end up staying with the guy who won you, so he's not been properly vetted yet."

"I don't think it's in the brother handbook that the younger one gets to have a say in what the older one does."

"Oh, really?" He'd moved to mocking me now. "I'm sure I can find where that is. Besides, I owe you. You've grilled every guy I've ever seen since I was fifteen."

Truth. I could be relentless where Bobby's dating choices were concerned—sometimes they were just not good. And I had that whole "man of the family" thing hanging over my head too.

"And look who you ended up with. Sebastian's awesome. And Kyle approved." I struggled not to laugh because this repeated so many arguments we'd had as teenagers. I wanted to see how far he'd go.

"I'm capable of making good decisions. He's proof of that."

"Yeah, after I rejected Corey, Zee, and Bryce, plus a few others. You made some really disturbing choices."

"Okay, first of all, Bryce was the first, and I didn't know what I was doing or what I wanted. Not to mention the fact that you frankly scared away Zee before I knew more than how good his blowjobs were."

"Trust me. That was probably all he was good for."

"Jerk." Bobby chuckled though, breaking our fake disagreement.

My phone beeped with an incoming call. My watch showed my agent's name. "Bobby, I gotta call you back. It's Candace."

"Oh, shit. I hope it's good news, bro."

"You and me both. I'll let you know."

I swiped to the other call and headed into my kitchen to grab a water. I needed to be on my feet for this call so I could pace if it went sideways.

"Hey, Candace. What's up?"

"Hey, Kyle, I wish I had better news." That's all it took for me to start walking between the living room, kitchen, and bedroom. "I just had an exploratory call with the Phoenix front office. I'd say it's all but done at this point since they talked to me about contract terms. I

142

wanted to let you know before anything made it into the press."

"Shit." I barely heard myself say it. I couldn't even muster anger at this point.

"I'm sorry, Kyle. I wish we had some control over it. I'll work to get you the best trade deal possible. I could try to make some noise to hold it up, but I'll be honest, I don't think you want that on your reputation. You're known as an easy-going player, doing what you need to do, supporting the team. In this case, you'd be doing the right thing for Detroit by exiting gracefully and being the guy Phoenix wants by coming in without a fuss."

Candace knew me well. Part of me wanted to rant, scream, and cry foul. She'd listen if I did that. Tantrums weren't really who I was though.

"What do you think we're looking at in terms of time? Are they gonna run up to the trade deadline or make it sooner?"

Despite asking, I wasn't sure I wanted to know. The trade deadline was weeks away, and if they were talking to Candace, I couldn't imagine either side waiting long.

"I expect sooner." Her computer chimed, and she clicked keys. "You going to be okay?"

"Yeah. I kinda have to be."

"Look, I know the timing's bad since you've got the new guy in your life." Of course Candace paid attention to my social when I dropped that kind of news. "If there's anything I can help with, let me know."

"I appreciate that. I've tried to make peace with it. Mom's prepared if I have to make a quick move. And Austin... Well, he's at least aware of the possibility. I'm doing my best not to worry about any of it."

"All right. I'll keep you posted."

"Thanks, Candace. We'll talk soon."

"Bye, Kyle."

She disconnected the call faster than I did. The universe didn't like me. Just as things started to click with Austin after last night a move looked even closer than before.

But last night...

We'd discovered that we spooned great, fitting perfectly without even really thinking about it. We'd left my house early this morning—I had to take him back to pick up his car so he could go home and get ready for work as I headed for practice.

We planned to hang out again tonight, but this time at his place to mix it up.

"What's the word?" Bobby got right to it as he answered my call back.

I relayed what Candace told me.

"I'm so sorry. I know it's not..."

"But I gotta buck up and deal with it. I can't jeopardize my career over it."

"What have you done with my brother?"

"I don't know what you're talking about," I deadpanned, imagining the look he'd level on me if we were face-to-face. "Look, I know how I've been about commitment to home and family, but you and Mom have worked to get me out of that. Frankly, being with Austin has helped that too. I can't create something new if I'm obsessed over some outdated, misplaced commitment. I'm trying to act my age instead of like an eight-year-old."

"Good for you." He meant it too. We both knew how to throw around bravado, but we also had our sincere voices, and that's what Bobby gave me. "What's Austin think about..."

"He knows. We haven't talked much about what it means." I sighed long and hard. "You know, maybe this is a sign I shouldn't be doing this with him."

"Don't say that. That's ridiculous."

We didn't speak for a moment. The only way I knew the call was still connected was I heard his TV in the background.

"Phoenix might be okay, right?" He tried for a silver lining.

"Seriously? They don't even do winter there. No frozen ponds for skating. And I'm sure you can't make a sandman."

"Well, I think that's probably just sand sculpture. You can work on those skills, I suppose. Of course, you'd have to have a good amount of water for that too. At least you'd have the major component of ice..."

I chuckled, and it quickly rolled into a hysterical laugh. Bobby joined in. The sandman thing wasn't all that funny, but the entire situation was hilarious in a tragic way. Might as well crack up over it.

"I needed that," I said once we both calmed down. "Thank you." I took a moment, deciding if I wanted to ask my next question—especially since I'd said I wanted to be a grown up.

"Is Mom really okay with the trade? I know she says that I don't need to worry..."

"I know you hold on to what everybody told you after dad's funeral for some twenty years, but Mom doesn't need a man of the family unless she decides to go find another one." Cue Bobby's empathetic therapist voice. "She's always said she had the love of her life, and even though it was only for a few years, she's never wanted anyone else."

This repeated many discussions we'd had, but I needed to hear it. "You're right. And I know I'm silly."

"No, you're not." I stopped pacing and dropped onto the couch—missing Austin nestled against me as he'd been last night. "What's silly is they dumped all that on you when you were eight. They thought they were giving you something to focus on. Don't get me wrong, I'm grateful that you felt like I was your responsibility. It kept us close. But you need to feel like you can go on to a new city and do whatever you want without worrying about Mom—or me." He paused, and I knew he had more to say. "Can I dispense a little advice you may not want?"

When he said it that way, I rarely wanted to hear what came next, even though he'd be right. "Give me your worst."

"Don't just turn Austin away. I saw the happiness in your eyes with that picture you posted. Let him have a say in what happens. Don't use the trade as the reason to call it off. And make sure if you're going to hold his work life against him that you actually talk about what all that means. You deserve what I've got with Seb, so please don't just give up."

I figured he'd say more about Mom. Bobby didn't catch me off guard much, but he got me by bringing up Austin in that context.

I couldn't debate anything he'd said—of course. "I'll think about it. I promise."

"I can't ask for more than that. Talk soon, okay, bro?"

"Thanks, Bobby. Love ya, man."

I had a lot to think about.

A lot of adulting lay ahead. I'd never been away from home for more than a month. Even for college, I was only in Ann Arbor; I could get home anytime I wanted to.

Of course Bobby and Mom didn't need me to take care of either one of them. One day hopefully that would sink into my thick skull.

It was less clear what to do about Austin though. Yesterday was perfect. Of course it couldn't always be that way, but he did seem to want to get away from being a total workaholic control freak. But, I had no idea how to manage something long distance because I hardly knew how to handle a relationship in the first place. At least we both had that problem.

If nothing else, I needed to update him on the news Candace gave me, so I shot him a text so he'd get it from me directly.

# TWENTY-TWO

## AUSTIN

"I DON'T UNDERSTAND how this can happen. We've got state-of-the-art security across the board. We pass security audits. How did our prototype end up with the competition?" My temple pulsed as a rage headache gripped me. Meanwhile, the knot in my stomach went from making me ill to wanting to punch something to release it. Forcing my voice to remain even rather than lashing out wasn't easy.

After the amazing afternoon and night with Kyle, I'd gotten a phone call from Tamara as I changed clothes to prepare to come back to the office. Tamara and I often talked in the morning as we commuted to get a head start on the day. She led with news that our prototype servers were breached. Everything we had out on review, including two new client pitches as well as new model year details for our existing ones, were stolen. Some had ended up on Twitter

I leveled my gaze at Max, the director of IT. "We know where it happened, but we're still not clear how"—he highlighted reports he had displayed on the big screen in my office—"a hack bypassed the security and copied everything out of the partition for the prototypes."

He took a breath and shifted to a new set of screens. I held back comments to let him finish.

"It appears to be a targeted job because the other partitions on the server where we've got the code that our clients actually use hasn't had any abnormal activity. What we're still working on is tracing the inbound and outbound traffic to see who did—"

I slammed my open hand on the table. Max and Tamara flinched. Momentarily, I felt bad because I didn't often lose my temper. Honestly, my staff didn't usually give me a reason to. This time, I couldn't hold back.

"The gap I see here," I said as I flipped screens on my tablet, "is how we allowed security to get so lapse and why we didn't detect the abnormal traffic."

"It's definitely a gap." The confidence he'd spoken with before diminished. "We're not sure if there's a bug in our security software or if it was somehow compromised. We should've known files were being accessed without the proper authorizations."

"How often do we review the security software and protocols?"

Max opened his mouth but closed it without speaking.

"We all know security is constantly patched as recommended by the vendor, and we do analysis every six months to make sure we're buttoned up." Tamara spoke up in her commanding but even tone, contrasting my anger. "We just passed our last audit less than three months ago."

"I'm preparing everything for the Michigan Cyber Command Center and the FBI in case our data crossed state lines." Max put up more info on the screen with the documents he'd assembled.

We'd worked with MC3 before when one of the car

companies we worked with had a hack. They'd been good in that case, and hopefully they would be here too.

"What about the innovation summit material?" I assumed that material was safe since it hadn't been called out.

"No evidence of tampering there," Max said, sounding relieved to deliver some good news.

At least our latest and greatest wasn't compromised.

"We'll figure out our next steps for Atlas," Tamara said. "It's not going to be an easy conversation with them since they had the most proprietary material in what was taken."

I'd gotten an earful from the CEO of Atlas shortly after Tamara called. "I don't know what they're going to come at us with. With their information ending up on Twitter, it blows their new model announcement out of the water. They made it clear that they'd be talking to counsel today on what their options were."

"I'd like to take the server completely offline," Max said. "Until we can ensure its security, I'd rather not have anything publicly available that carries our critical materials."

"Fine." That answer was easy. "Do what you need to do to fully investigate how this happened and to make sure it can't happen again. Let the delivery team know the best way to move code around in the short term if we need to."

"Will do." Max got up. "I'll get that done now."

He headed out, and I rubbed my forehead. A pounding headache formed behind my eyes. I couldn't have seen this coming, and yet my brain ran at breakneck speed trying to figure out how I could've prevented it.

The company was already on shaky ground as we tried to win Atlas, and now they had no reason to trust us.

"I can tell what you're thinking." Tamara put her tablet

down, stood, and went to the shelf where I kept a couple of bottles. She poured some bourbon for us. "No matter how much time you spent on work, you couldn't have found this."

She returned to the table and set a glass down. Wordlessly, I raised it to her and she did the same with her own. We downed the brown liquid. It burned and warmed as it went down.

"It doesn't mean it's not some kind of karma coming after me for letting my focus waver."

"Really?" Her serious face broke to give me the smirk I'd seen a lot in college. "I'm sure the karma goddess has better things to do than come after you for maybe having a life outside of this place."

She knew exactly the right thing to say, even if I didn't fully believe it. My way of living worked for years, but when I tried to do things differently, something comes along that can wreck everything faster than not securing a client.

"Want to divide and conquer for the day?" I asked since I had no comeback for her take on karma.

"Let's do it." We picked up our tablets at the same time. She had her tapping finger ready to go. "I'll huddle with P.R. next. We're going to get a lot of questions from what was out there briefly, so I'll make sure we're buttoned up on responses. I'll work with Donovan to create talking points too since we might both end up doing some interviews."

I nodded. Tamara always ran with public relations because that was so much easier for her to manage. "I'll get the details on the other clients affected and set up meetings. Let's find out from Max what's going to need to happen with the investigations too. No doubt one of us has to liaison with the agencies."

"Let's meet back here at twelve thirty and debrief." She clicked off her tablet and got up. "We got this."

She didn't believe it even as she said it. We both needed to be more convincing to be able to sell that idea.

Tamara exited and left my door open, which was standard for when I was in here by myself.

I leaned back in my chair and let it tip back farther.

Pulling away even the slightest bit that I had had been a mistake. Even before this, the company hadn't been as secure as it could've been.

How did I fool myself into thinking Kyle would be good for me? The focus needed to stay on work to ensure AMDD had a secure future—if any future at all.

I sat forward and grabbed my tablet. Bringing up Slack, I messaged Jack so he'd have instructions at the ready as soon as he arrived. *Good morning. Please set meetings with each of the department heads for today. I want complete status reports. Also please get me a flight, leaving as late tonight as possible, to get me to New York so I can be in meetings first thing tomorrow.*

I moved on to an email. I needed to schedule with Atlas to try to salvage the disaster. Emails needed to go out to the other clients on that server so I could talk to them as well.

The phone buzzed and brought me out of my message composition.

Kyle.

I shouldn't, but I wanted to see him and have a moment to talk to somebody separated from this. And maybe get a hug. Kyle had a way of calming me by just being him.

Yet, the distraction possibility was too much.

Another buzz.

I flipped it face down on the table. A wave of sadness washed over me as I reconsidered it.

I wasn't boyfriend material.

I was barely CEO material at the moment.

Writing the best email ever had my focus—something that let Atlas know we took the matter seriously. State and federal agencies were alerted and that the matter had my full attention.

# TWENTY-THREE

## KYLE

"Not a peep in two days?" Mom asked.

She sat across the kitchen island as we both drank coffee. One of our longest traditions was to get together once a week and have coffee or maybe hot chocolate.

We'd started the tradition during high school. There had been so much going as she worked and Bobby and I had sports and after-school stuff that she'd wanted to make sure there was time to catch up. She'd done the same with Bobby —and still did, but now it happened on FaceTime.

Mine would be on FaceTime soon probably. Our standing time was Sunday morning if I was in town. Austin dominated today's conversation.

"He texted me late Thursday that he had to go to New York for an emergency meeting. He told me the company was having... How did he put it?" I thought back to the night we'd had together. "Difficulties. I've texted him and know he's getting the messages because they change to *read* at some point." The memories flooded in, and I wanted him back so bad in that moment. "That afternoon and night had been so perfect. I can't imagine why he'd ghost me like this."

I sounded more emotional than I'd intended, but I had a hard time holding back with Mom. It didn't help that she fixed me with her best concerned look. Usually it was reserved for when I felt like I'd messed up a game. There were similarities, though, since I'd clearly done something wrong here.

"Maybe he's not ignoring you. It could be he just got super busy and hasn't been able to tell you yet. I will say that you two seemed to have a good connection. I know you haven't seen each other very long, but... I've never seen you like that with anyone. Just the way you were when you were here. You two had a vibe."

"Oh, Mom. A vibe? What does that even mean?" My face heated, and that meant at least a faint blush in my cheeks. Talking to Bobby about guys was weird enough sometimes, but with Mom...

"Now don't go doing that. I know all of your moods, and honestly, I liked seeing this new version of happy on you."

"New version of happy?" I grabbed another cinnamon roll from the box that I'd picked up on the way over. I took a bite so I didn't have to talk.

She nodded. "There's a particular way you are on the ice and when your content around me and Bobby. You had something else with Austin. You stole looks at him like I used to do with your father."

Wow. Like her and Dad. That was a major compliment.

"Maybe it's for the best. I told Bobby that I didn't know what to do if... or I guess when... I move to Phoenix. Maybe Austin's decided. I'd texted him the update on the trade. That could've been his tipping point."

I took a sip to give myself a moment.

"I'm not going to defend his actions because going quiet

is certainly rude." She grabbed the coffee pot and topped us off. The lines deepened across her forehead as her concern increased, and that pushed a wave of sadness through me. I hadn't meant to bring us down this morning.

"How did you know when you met Dad that he was, you know, the one?"

"The unhelpful answer is that I just knew." Mom smiled, that one she saved for thinking about Dad. It used to have a sadness to it, but for the last five years or so, it was the smile of happy memories. "Have I ever told you how your dad and I met?"

I shook my head. I'd heard a lot of stories about the two of them as a couple but never how they met. How had I gone so long without that story?

"There was a band. Pretty popular one that played different places on campus. I'd gone out on a Thursday night. It was late because they had the closing slot. No one wanted to go with me, but I didn't let that deter me. Admittedly not the best idea to go out to a bar, even on a safe campus, by myself super late. But I was young and stupid."

She paused, drank some more coffee, and shifted her gaze out the glass doors that led to the patio, as if the memory was out there.

"The concert was great. I had fun. I danced. I sang along way too loudly. I didn't drink because I had the good sense not to drink by myself and then have to drive back to the dorm. After the last song, I headed out. Somebody followed me. Something was creepy about the guy from the start. He wanted to treat me to a nightcap or something. I kept saying no and regretting some of my choices for the night."

Tendrils of anger tickled the back of my brain. It didn't

matter that this had happened decades ago. Someone had messed with Mom, and I didn't like that.

"The guy kept pushing and getting more frustrated. All of a sudden, your father showed up. He'd just gotten off work from the diner down the street. He got between me and the guy and told him that he needed to back off." Laughter crept into her voice. "Your father in college was not the strong guy you boys knew. He was scrawny, a bean-pole, and totally adorable."

She put her hand over her mouth like she shouldn't say that. I put my hand on her other one as she relived the moment. I knew she loved Dad; it radiated from her as she told the story.

"This guy was probably half a foot taller than Marcus and clearly worked out. But your dad had no hesitation. He stood his ground until the guy's bluster wore out and he stalked off. He then introduced himself and asked if he could follow me home to make sure that guy didn't. He didn't leave until I was safely in the building."

The tremor in her hand spoke to the emotion she felt.

"That's amazing. I always knew he was good with people. He seemed to be able to handle any situation. I was aware of that even as a kid."

She nodded. "That was your father. I didn't even see him again for, like, three weeks. We ended up at the library at the same time. He was studying at one of the tables, and I went over with the intention of just thanking him again for his help and to see if I could buy him a coffee or something. As soon as he looked at me with those sky blue eyes... I felt it right here." She put her free hand over her heart and patted her chest. "On our six-month anniversary, he said my smile at the library had undone him. It was love on second sight for us."

God, I wished they were still together. Her wistful look made goose bumps form over my arms and threatened to push too many emotional buttons.

"How come you never told that before?"

She gave a slight shrug "Some memories seem more personal. But it answered your question, so it was time." She shifted her hand from under mine to on top. "You'll know when it happens. Trust me and trust yourself. You'll know it at the very deepest fiber of your being. I know that's cheesy, but it's true."

Damn. Austin had rooted himself pretty firmly in my heart. My practical side protested. It didn't fit with me leaving or with the way he ran his life.

"If you have strong feelings for him, you need to let him know." Like a mom, she knew exactly where my thoughts were. "You can both decide to break it off, but you can't leave it hanging. You'll both be miserable."

I couldn't argue with her logic or the battle going on in my head over what I wanted versus what I thought the right answer was.

"Remember, people spend time apart. Your father traveled a lot for work. Phoenix doesn't have to be the end for you two. Let's not forget, neither of you are exactly strapped for cash." The amused, knowing look made me chuckle and shake my head. Mom was not subtle. "You could easily have a home here and there. There are a million ways it can work."

"This is why I like coffee time—getting a ton of wisdom from Mom."

"Anytime." She put another cinnamon roll on each plate. I hadn't even realized I'd managed to devour the one I'd had while she talked.

Mom talks solved so much. I needed to figure out what

Austin and I meant to each other and how his silence factored into it.

# TWENTY-FOUR

## AUSTIN

FOUR DAYS in New York and nothing to show for it. It didn't matter how many meetings I had or how many documents I produced on our security and some of the initial findings from MC3, which agreed with our assessment of an attack from IPs in China that are often linked to industrial espionage. We learned a lot about upgrades to our systems to prevent and alert to such attacks, but it was too late.

Atlas refused to consider us further as a partner and continued to threaten legal action against AMDD since their proprietary information had been compromised.

I couldn't blame them.

Infuriated didn't begin to cover how our board of directors reacted. Tamara and I were under fire for not having better IT protocols and not doing a lot more to shore up our customer's concerns.

The board was justified in their feelings. This could really sink the ship. Atlas wasn't the only deal we'd hoped to close soon, but now we were distracted, cleaning up this mess instead of pushing forward. All of our prospects and clients now had reason to be suspect of how we protected relationships.

A message came up on my computer.

Damn.

I'd had my texts coming in on my screen to ensure I didn't miss anything as I worked to stay in touch with clients and staff the past few days.

*I miss you.*

He'd sent that at least once a day, and sometimes he'd send other news too.

Given the time, he was probably still at the arena and in the locker room. I'd kept up with the game—another win for the team, including a goal for Kyle.

God, I missed him. Missed how I felt around him.

I'd needed the break to focus though. I couldn't allow myself to get swept up again.

My heart took over and replied even while the work-obsessed side said not to.

*I miss you too. I'm sorry I disappeared.*

Three dots instantly appeared, and I waited for the words to come back.

*OMG! It's so good to hear from you. I thought you might never speak to me again. Where are you?*

Talking over text made this an easier conversation.

*About ninety minutes out from Detroit. Flying home from NYC.*

I imagined Kyle in front of his locker, sitting on the bench, fresh out of the shower and wrapped in a towel as droplets of water cascaded down his chest.

*Good trip? I hit the road tomorrow for a couple days, which you probably know. Want to come over after you land? Love to see you.*

*You played good tonight. Congrats on the goal.* I added

the hockey stick and net emojis while avoiding his invitation and question about the trip.

*Thanks. Want to contribute here as long as I can.*

Crap. He must be resigned to the idea at this point. He'd told me the latest from his agent before I'd left on this trip.

I'd been a shit boyfriend. I'd done nothing to reach out, see how he was, how his family was. Forget being a boyfriend, I didn't act like a good friend. Period.

*Keep it up. Your biggest fan appreciates it.*

My lame response got me a simple smile emoji back.

Then he launched into something longer. The dots kept going. Sometimes they'd disappear for a moment and then start again. I waited him out.

*Did I do something wrong? You've been quiet for days. I probably shouldn't do this over text but the silence freaked me out. We had such a good night. Can we at least talk? I'd like to figure out what we are before the trade actually happens. If you still think there's an us. You know I'll be up for a few hours coming off the game and honestly I can sleep on the trip tomorrow. If you don't want to come over, meet up for a late night breakfast?*

Fuck.

I'd really done a number on him. I didn't realize that behind all the simple hello texts he felt like this. More to beat myself up about alongside everything else.

Did I put myself out there for him tonight or did I defer until he got back? That would only buy me three or four days since it was only two East Coast games.

I owed both of us to make it tonight.

*Late breakfast sounds good. I can come directly to your place if you want.*

*Cool! Look forward to seeing you. I'll whip up pancakes*

*using my mom's recipe so they'll be hella good. Spoiler alert: there's bacon inside. See you in a couple hours or so.*

Bacon infused pancakes. Well damn.

*I'll be there as fast as I can.* I capped that off with an airplane, car, and smiley emoji.

At least if our relationship ended, it'd be over what I imagined would be an amazing meal.

I didn't know how we could keep this going. I didn't know how to be the man Kyle deserved. With the trade, at least he'd be in a new place to start again. Although that meant no family around him, which he'd hate.

I couldn't think about this without making my head hurt with regret.

The more I considered it, the more I didn't know how we'd escape with our hearts intact.

# TWENTY-FIVE

## KYLE

HE'D RESPONDED!

After so many days, a single sentence postgame somehow shook out a response.

And what the hell was I doing, pouring my heart out in a text?

We needed to talk. Was this the right way to go?

Neutral territory might've been a better idea than my kitchen.

Time ticked down. My defenses had to be up so I wouldn't say a bunch of nice things and then convince him to make out—which I really wanted. A serious talk had to happen though.

Maybe management could walk in and tell me I had to go to Phoenix immediately. Do not pass go. Do not collect your potential boyfriend. Go be a center in another state. Thank you and goodbye. That would be the only thing that could extract me from what I'd signed myself up for.

I finished getting cleaned up, and no escape hatch appeared. With no other choice, I headed home. No sooner was I in the car and I got fidgety, my fingers tapping against the steering wheel while my left leg bounced.

At home, I tidied up what little there was to put away— a few stray dishes in the sink and some mail that was spread across the coffee table. Prepping the food relaxed me a bit. The bacon needed to be cooked and cooled so it could be chopped before going into the pancake batter.

What possessed me to send that message? So freaking stupid.

The consolation was that we'd soon know where we stood.

As I cooked up way more bacon than I needed, my phone chirped.

*Walking through the airport now. Need me to pick up anything?*

It'd be embarrassing if I said no only to discover that I indeed needed something, but my quick inventory showed everything was here.

*Nope. All good. See you when you get here.*

I grabbed a few strips of that extra bacon and chowed down. The postgame hunger creeped in, and nobody was going to miss them.

*Great. Be there soon.*

Did I need to change clothes? As soon as I'd gotten home, I stripped out of my suit—no way I'd cook in that. But were sweats the best choice?

I headed to the bedroom. I couldn't cook anything else until Austin arrived. My nerves had me overthinking everything. Sweats were fine. He'd seen me in sweats before. This wasn't a date. We were eating and talking.

I straightened the bed up since I'd not made it this morning. Silly since we had no business ending up back here. Still, I fussed with everything.

The doorbell rang. He'd made good time.

Crap.

Shoes or no shoes. Were socked feet okay?

Overthinking again. My house. I was comfortable after game. I laughed nervously at myself.

I headed for the door quickly; he didn't need to think I wanted him to freeze out there.

Damn. He looked amazing. He clearly went directly to the airport after his meetings because he was in one of his good suits. No tie but the jacket, shirt, and pants fit him just so, perfectly highlighting the geek I'd already fallen for.

More importantly, he looked exhausted and, worse, defeated. What had been going on?

"I'm glad you messaged." He turned to look at me as I closed the door.

Should I hug him? Frustration rose in my gut—I hated all the questions.

"I'm sorry I've been quiet. It was a jerk move."

"I could've done more than just text too. I could've found out from Jack where you were and came to you."

Sad laughter followed.

He made the decision on the hug, closing the distance between us and wrapping me tight. I didn't hold back and wrapped my arms around him. The faintest whiff of his cologne remained, probably left over from when he got dressed this morning. He relaxed as his entire body unclenched and his shoulders dropped.

"Are you okay?"

"Yeah. It's just been..." If he wanted to continue, he could, and I'd hold him for as long as he wanted. "I'm just happy to see you," he said after a moment. With that, he loosened his hug, and I did the same so it wouldn't get awkward.

He forced a smile as he stepped back, but his eyes didn't contain the same emotion. He was holding something back —whether it was about us or work…?

"Let's cook." I shifted us to something safer.

"Yes." He followed me to the kitchen as he talked. "Have you at least eaten something? After all, I know how you get postgame."

"I might've eaten some of the bacon."

"Can't go wrong with that." He slipped off his suit coat and draped it over one of the chairs at the breakfast bar. "Is there anything I can do?"

"Want to scramble the eggs?

"That I can do. It's one of the few culinary skills I have. I can also make toast. Anything else might get a little out of control."

"Good to know." I took stuff out of the fridge as he hovered around the edge of the counter near the stove. "I'll get a little bit ahead on the pancakes, then you can do that." I busied myself with a large mixing bowl, the one Mom had given me a few years back specifically for pancakes. "What sent you off to New York so quickly?"

"A lot went wrong Thursday morning. I went for some meetings, hoping to fix it." Out of nowhere, he started a pot of coffee. It'd go great with the food, but I hadn't expected him to just do it. My heart did a somersault. This was a flash of what life could be like, making food and talking at the end of a day. "I failed though."

The tension returned to his shoulders.

"Is the company going to be okay?" Part of me didn't want to know because knowing would only draw us closer together rather than separating. Still, I knew how important this was, and I couldn't avoid the question.

He looked at me, and for a moment, I thought he might cry. "I don't know. It's pretty bad. Most of our clients and prospects are extremely unhappy."

Knowing how he thought, I didn't have to make much of a leap to know that he completely blamed himself.

"Tamara and I have an emergency meeting with the board tomorrow. The bad news will outweigh the good."

I reached out and gave him a quick embrace. The company meant the world to him. I bit back my reflex response that everything would be okay.

I sighed, frustrated on his behalf. "What will the board do?"

I went back to getting the batter together, but I made sure to pay attention as he talked.

"The company is set up in thirds. I have a third, Tamara has a third, and the people that make up the board have the rest. This could get interesting because Tamara and I have majority when we're agreeing with each other. It gets more interesting if we don't because the board can sway the outcome. It's rare that Tamara and I disagree. But with everything that's happened, I honestly don't know. The board could justifiably decide to oust me, and if Tamara agreed..."

He looked like emotions might explode out of him. His voice remained even, but the stress was etched deep in the lines around his eyes and on his forehead.

"I have no idea what to say. I know I can't make it better or make it go away."

"To be honest with you, being with you helps. I can't explain it, but you calm me down."

Dropping the whisk in the batter mid-stir, I went and pulled him in close for a good, proper hug. He laid his head against my chest, and I just held him. We stayed that way for a few minutes until he pulled back and looked up and me.

"As much as this is wonderful, I'd really like some food. The lingering bacon smell is really making me hungry."

We chuckled, and I gave him one last squeeze. "Fair enough. Nothing quite like that smell to kick in the hungry."

I popped the oven on warm and set my large skillet—also a gift from Mom—on a burner. "I'm thinking be ready to scramble eggs in about fifteen minutes."

"I saw some sausage in your fridge. Any chance we can cook up some of that too?"

"More pork is never wrong."

We fell into a good rhythm. He cooked sausage while I made pancakes. He'd open the oven and slide out the rack so I could add to the ones warming. When it was time, he got the eggs going.

Again, all this was a flash of what a future could be. He'd be in more comfortable clothes. There might even be a kid. A wave of sadness rolled through me since this seemed unattainable with him.

It didn't take long to have the meal ready and laid out across the breakfast bar. We sat at the corner so we were close—our knees touching—and could look at each other.

We ate in silence for a few minutes. Unlike our first postgame meal, I kept myself from devouring everything at once. Although he did eat at a good clip himself.

"This is really good. Once again, your mom comes through."

"Yeah. She's awesome." I sighed as nerves clinched my chest. I couldn't delay anymore. "I have to ask, what happened? I didn't hear from you at all. We went from an amazing night to dead silence."

Now he released a heavy sigh.

Here we go.

# TWENTY-SIX

## AUSTIN

He locked eyes with me. Could I just say nothing and eat?

Of course not.

After his amazing hug, talking about my withdrawal became more difficult.

"I... I... pulled back." Fuck that. I couldn't let the anxiety get the better of me and retreat to stumbling over words. "It wasn't right. You deserved to know where my head was, but I put everything I had into work. You know how important it is to me and how the thought of losing it terrifies me, which is exactly where I'm at right now. I lost focus... and I have no idea what to do."

He looked like I'd punched him. The bit of a smile he'd had disappeared, and a storm rolled through his beautiful eyes.

"I don't know what to do now." The speed that the words spilled out of my mouth increased. "There are parts of us that are so good together. You calm me down, make me happy. I want that, but I don't know if I can have a boyfriend and a company. I know that's sappy, but it's how I feel."

He almost opened his mouth, but I plowed ahead, afraid that if I stopped before I said it all that I'd chicken out.

"So much of me wants us to work. But I don't know how to give you the boyfriend you deserve. And I know I should let some of the work go for my sanity. I know that here." I tapped on my head and then my heart. "But there's a part" —I tapped on my head again—"terrified about getting into a position where I can't take care of the people that are important."

My fork rattled against the plate as my hand shook. I talked okay, but other parts of me were freaking out.

Kyle kept his eyes trained on me. I suppose I should be glad that he hasn't already decided that we're done. The very thing he'd been worried about—the job, lack of attention, all of it—was happening.

"We've got the same problems," Kyle said, and I raised my eyebrows in surprise. "Phoenix looms. It's just a matter of time. And then what? As much as I don't want to leave home, I'm not gonna have a choice unless I walk away from my career, and, of course, I'm not going to do that. But me in Phoenix and you in Detroit. How is that good for us? Especially since we're barely a couple. And I haven't exactly been totally fair to you. You built AMDD from the ground up. How can I expect you to give me more attention than you give that? I was a shit even suggesting it."

The Phoenix thing hadn't seemed as huge as my problem, but I saw his point. And his apology—the thing was, he'd pegged me right. Outside of another workaholic, no one was going to appreciate my work style. "I would say people make it work long-distance, but I don't even know what that would look like with our schedules."

Kyle nodded and dropped his gaze to his plate. He moved around a couple of the sausage links. "We're both pretty royally fucked on this one."

I grunted and took a big bite of pancake followed by some sausage. "Has Greta ever considered infusing these pancakes with sausage too? The combination with syrup is damn good."

The rapid topic shift didn't faze him. "She's done that a couple times. She's never happy with how big the sausage ends up. Sometimes I just do a roll up." He took one of the sausages, wrapped the pancake around it, swirled it in the syrup on his plate, and took a big bite. "It's not exactly the proper way to eat these, and it can be far from tidy. Mom is probably twitching in her sleep right now because I've just done this when I'm eating with someone else."

We laughed while I did exactly what he'd done. It was perfection. We ate a couple more pancakes the same way.

"How do we do this?" My voice broke. I hated that even though it perfectly expressed the situation.

"We can at least stay friends, right?" Kyle looked at me earnestly.

"I... um..." My thoughts scattered. I didn't know how to finish that.

"Or we become boyfriends who have to live in different places." I wasn't ready for that answer. "We see each other as often as we can. You managed to come see me in Vegas. I've certainly got the means to travel. I'll be here during the off-season for sure. We keep going and see what happens. If we both want it, we should be able to figure it out. "

Maybe all wasn't lost.

"I know I haven't been the best." I fought against looking somewhere else.

"And I haven't been the most flexible either."

175

"I won't go silent again." Quiet hadn't done either of us any good, and I wouldn't do that again.

"Good. That was the worst."

"For what it's worth, I felt bad every time I saw one of your messages."

We exhaled at the same time. He looked at me with the sweetest gaze, which quickened my pulse.

"I'd been so worried about this talk." Kyle sounded relieved, which unlocked some of my tension even as the board meeting loomed. "More breakfast? It's too good not to finish."

"Yes, please."

Impulsively, I grabbed his hand and kissed his knuckles. He tasted like syrup since it'd been the hand he held the pancake with.

We grabbed more of everything and kept eating—except we smiled as we went instead of wearing various looks of dread. The board meeting would be what it was, but I had Kyle again, and that made whatever came next okay.

We finished a crazy amount of food. I'm not sure where I put all of it. While Kyle was refueling from the game, the meal was far bigger than my usual.

Before we could utter a word after the feast, we yawned simultaneously.

"Do you want to crash here?" Kyle asked. That was a surprise.

"I'd love to. I've got to get up early though. It'll mean an early alarm."

He leaned in and brushed my cheek with a kiss.

"That's okay. Like I said, I can catch more sleep on the flight to Dallas."

I cleared the dishes to the sink. As the hot water flowed, I swirled some soap from the dispenser onto the plates.

"Leave those. I can clean up in the morning."

"No can do. I heard something recently that the rule was whoever didn't cook had to do the dishes, and I think you did most of the cooking."

"I think it was more equal. I'll help."

*Comfort.* The word kept bouncing around in my head. It defined the evening. Just being with Kyle, sharing meals, keeping house. I wanted to make this work.

The cleanup took no time, and I followed Kyle as he turned off lights.

"Do you want to shower or anything?" Kyle asked.

"I'm really pretty wiped. Can we just fall into bed?"

"More than okay."

Kyle slipped out of his sweats but stayed in blue boxer briefs. I went down to my boxers too, and we got in on opposite sides of the bed but met in the middle, just like the other night.

I lay on my back, and Kyle wrapped his big, strong arm across my chest. He snuggled his head against my shoulder, planting a couple of kisses. I craned my head to put some on his forehead.

I wanted to do more, but the exhaustion, combined with all the food, wouldn't allow it. Instead, I happily drifted off, nestled in close.

# TWENTY-SEVEN

## KYLE

I HATED that I had to leave after our breakfast. Waking up together started my day off great though. We cleaned up, had coffee, and then headed out. The Arsenal practiced at home and then flew to Dallas for a night game, which we lost.

Austin and I texted during the days of the trip and talked before we went to sleep. It was fun FaceTiming while we both lay in bed. He worried about the company and his ability to fix what had happened. He didn't share details, which I both understood and appreciated since I wasn't sure I'd get the nuances. He invited me to come speak about leadership and community at the innovation summit that was coming up, and I said yes. If he wanted me there and he thought it could help, I'd gladly do it.

We stayed away from heavy relationship stuff, which was probably for the best. Those things were better done in person, and we both seemed on the same page with that without so much as an awkward attempt at it.

Tonight, we played, and that meant sharing the ice with Garrett.

G and I messed with each other relentlessly during the game. I made one goofy face at him as we lined up for a face-off, and that set the tone for the entire game—faces and jokey trash talk when we were in earshot. It wasn't bad sportsmanship, although the refs did keep an eye on us because the occasional outbursts of laughter was quite unusual.

During the second intermission, David told me that the local sports network actually wanted me and G for an interview since it was clear that, while there was a rivalry between the teams and a serious game going on, we'd obviously been friends forever and knew how to have fun. We'd squared off dozens of times over the years and had never messed around like this before, but I had a ball with it, and I knew he did too.

I'm sure I liked it more than he did because the Arsenal led the game.

"If you're gonna move that slow, ESPN might take you off that cover," I quipped to G as he failed to catch me on a breakaway. His goalie covered the shot so I didn't feel too bad about harassing him more in the final minutes of the game.

"I didn't get that cover for speed. So just keep talking. I might use this body to knock you on your ass." He passed super close to me so a ref wouldn't hear and take it as an actual threat. It didn't matter, though, since that was our last shift before the final buzzer.

After the stars of the game were announced, G and I would return to the ice to talk to the reporter. Since I wasn't a star, I went to the locker room, stored my stick, and tried to arrange my hair so it wouldn't totally look like helmet head.

David waited by the door, checking his phone and waiting for the message that it was time for the interview.

"Great job tonight, guys," Coach said as he came in. "Another all-important win toward locking in a playoff slot." He came over to me. "KP, can I grab you for a minute?"

This was it.

The bottom dropped out of my stomach, and I fought to control any emotions from peeking out.

The locker room got quiet because we all knew what was coming.

I struggled to keep it together—the mix of sadness and anger tried to overwhelm me. The fiery angry surprised me because I thought I'd worked through that already.

"Coach," David said, falling in step next to us, "he's about to do a quick TV segment—"

"Sorry. We need to see him before he goes on air. You'll have to delay or cancel if you need to."

"Hang tight. We'll do it as soon as I'm done. I'm not going to miss the chance to harass Garrett on TV." Thankfully, I sounded more confident than I felt.

David nodded and broke away.

"It's happened?" I asked.

"'Fraid so. Papers got signed during the game."

We arrived at an office, probably one they got permission to use to deliver the news. Coach closed the door behind us and pulled his phone from his pocket. He tapped the screen and faced it toward him.

"I've got Kyle here."

"Thanks." I recognized the GM's voice. Coach handed the phone over with the boss's face filling the screen, and I held it in front of me. "Hello, Kyle. Great game tonight. It was fun watching you and Howell snipe at each other."

"Thank you, sir." I couldn't suppress a grin, knowing we'd entertained at least one person besides ourselves.

"I imagine you know why we're talking."

I nodded.

"You, along with Helson and Feldman, are going to Phoenix where you'll play tomorrow night. Billington will be on our lineup for our next game as well."

Lucky him. He'd get an extra day to travel, unlike the three of us.

I nodded, managing to keep my sigh inside.

"I know this wasn't what you wanted. Phoenix, however, really wanted you, and we couldn't shake them off that. I imagine you know the impact Billington can have here."

"Yes, sir. I do."

"Your agent and the league will be in touch on all the logistics. The stuff in your locker here is getting packed up, and it'll meet you in Phoenix. There's a charter waiting for you at the airport, and someone from the team will meet you when you land. I'll be honest, I hope we get you home someday, even more so because we all know Detroit is where you want to be. If there's anything we can do during the transition, please let us know."

"I'll do that. Thank you."

"I know you've got an interview waiting, so I'll let you get to that. Thank you again, Kyle. It's been a pleasure having you on the Arsenal."

I nodded and handed the phone back to Coach. "I'll get Helson and be back in a moment." He tapped the screen and pocketed it. "It's been great working with you all these years."

"You too. I learned a lot." We did a bro hug and a hand-shake before going back into the hall.

David hovered just outside the door, and we headed back to the ice.

I joined G, standing just on the edge of the ice. Burlington's Coach was doing his postgame interview, and we waited to go next.

"You okay? I heard." G wrapped his arm around my shoulders.

I sighed. "Eh. I suppose I'm glad the hammer's finally dropped. I wish my last game was in Detroit. At least I got to play my last Arsenal game against you, so there's something."

"When do you go?"

I gave him all the details, and his expression clouded. I knew why. He expected me to freak all the more because I didn't get to go home first. I wanted to have a tantrum but I couldn't. I had to be an adult, a professional. The eight-year-old inside could do his thing later.

"I know Matty Berkshire pretty well. He used to play here. I'll give him a call. He's a good guy and grinds away on D. He's been there three years now."

"Thanks, man."

A woman did a walking slide across the ice to us from where the camera crew was. G greeted the reporter warmly. Not surprising they knew each other.

"They've just gone to commercial, and you guys are next. Let's get you over there." We followed. "The segment'll be two to three minutes. We're going to focus mostly on the fun you two had tonight, but we're gonna ask about the trade that just went down if that's okay, Kyle."

"Sure."

"There's always some friendly trash talk when we play against each other." G started us off after the intro. "Something about tonight... I don't know."

"Right? We got goofy." We looked at each other and couldn't hold straight faces. "We'd even grabbed lunch today so we'd caught up. Something about seeing him in our first faceoff just made me throw him a smirk and..."

"And we were off from there."

"Exactly."

We went on to talk a little about having a friendship that lasted more than a decade with hockey as the background.

I got a couple softball questions about the trade. "I'd like to thank all of the Arsenal fans, coaching staff, and the front office for giving the first seven years of my career a great start." I spoke from the heart, knowing this would end up rebroadcast in Detroit. "This trade is good for Detroit. As a longtime fan of the team, I know that. I hope to return one day. But for now, I'm off to Phoenix, where I'll give them my best."

"Phoenix is lucky to have this one," G said before the reporter could ask anything else. "He works hard, and he's an excellent competitor. It's a lot more fun to play with him than against him. That's something I know all too well. I look forward to making the cross-country trip in a few weeks to check him out in his new home."

I bumped G in the shoulder for making this more emotional than I had intended.

The reporter wrapped it up and threw back to the studio. "Thank you both for the time. And for some fun times on the ice tonight."

Headed back to the tunnel, we kept a slow pace. G asked, "You have time to grab a beer or something before you go?"

"I don't think so. There's a charter taking us tonight, but I don't know timing."

"No pressure. You know where to find me if you've got

time to kill. And it goes without saying, you can call me anytime."

We bumped fists, shot our hands backwards for the explosion, and then hugged.

Locker room chatter ran high. Helson and Feldman were surrounded. They'd been on the team a season and a half. As soon as I began stripping off my gear, guys drifted my way too. Lots of shaking hands, pats on the back, and all the stuff that happens when you don't get time for a more proper goodbye. The team promised a proper farewell party the next time I was in town.

Once the guys dispersed, Kennedy sat next to me. "Adriana texted and wanted me to tell you that she's going to miss you. She'll make sure your picture gets packaged for shipping to get to Phoenix so you'll have a little bit of home."

I nodded. I hadn't taken ownership yet since the show ran another couple of weeks. "I appreciate that."

"If there's anything we can do to help, let us know."

We stood and embraced. "Thanks. It's been great playing with you."

"Thirty minutes until we leave!" Jerry, the equipment manager, bellowed from the doorway, kicking everybody into overdrive.

"Shit. I gotta get moving. See you in a few weeks across the dot."

We had another back-slapping hug.

I hoped someone would show up with details on what we needed to do. Helson and Feldman were dressed and glued to their phones, so I stripped and headed for the shower.

Once the soothing, warm water rained down on me, my facade crumbled a little. A wave of emotions started in the pit of my stomach and vibrated into my chest. I hated every bit of this—not just the move, but that it happened here. A couple of deep breaths helped center me... barely.

The world wouldn't fall apart.

Mom would be fine.

Bobby would be fine.

Austin and I knew this was coming, and we'd be...

On the way to the airport, I'd call Mom. I probably had a message from her because she would've watched the game and heard the news. Even if she hadn't seen my interview, the commentators surely mentioned it.

I'd message Austin too. We'd have to sort out the innovation summit I was supposed to speak at because I didn't know if that'd be possible. Maybe I could get back for that and to get some of my stuff. Despite the water temperature, I shuddered.

"Hey, KP," Jerry called from the shower room entrance, "a car's here for you guys. It's waiting by the buses, and they'll go when you're ready. I put an envelope of itinerary information in your locker too."

"Thanks, Jerry. I don't know what I'm gonna do without you to keep me on track."

"You're welcome. I packed your gear too. Make sure they get that to the rink to wash right away. No time to do it here. Take care, man."

"Thanks again."

No reply likely meant he'd moved on to the next task of getting the team out of here.

I scrubbed quickly, even though I'd be happy to stay right here and not deal with any of this. That kid I kept tucked away near my heart pushed hard to be let loose.

When I got to my locker, only my suit hung there, my gear in its bag and my luggage sitting next to it.

I grabbed my phone. Mom had messaged. She'd seen the news and said I could call tonight if I needed to or we could talk tomorrow. I texted back in case she was still awake and let her know I'd call tomorrow. Bobby had messaged too with a similar text.

Austin had messaged too. A simple open-mouthed emoji.

Wow was an appropriate reaction.

*Hey. I don't get to come home. I play in Phoenix tomorrow night. I'll figure out what this means to my schedule and the summit. I miss you so bad and I'm pissed I don't get to see you tomorrow. Gotta get dressed since the ride to the airport is here.* I capped the message with my usual kissey face and heart.

Despite telling myself for days I was prepared for this, my heart was heavy because I wasn't going home. It took all my strength to hold back tears as I followed Helson and Feldman out.

# TWENTY-EIGHT

## AUSTIN

I HAD BARELY TOUCHED my dinner, and now that I had to make remarks, I thought I might throw up even though I'd eaten so little. Normally, I enjoyed these summits. The afternoon had gone well—at least, I thought it had. Tamara had other thoughts based on the meetings she'd had, and the evening had gone from one problem to another.

As I talked in a group with the chief of technical innovation for General Motors, Jack gave me a thumbs up from across the room. Kyle's plane had finally landed, but no way he'd get here in time to do our presentation.

As if on cue, Tamara appeared at my side. "I'm so sorry to interrupt, but I need to borrow Austin for a moment."

Tendrils of anxiety spread through my chest. Even though it didn't directly relate to our business, Kyle not being here to speak would reflect on me. It didn't matter that he'd been pulled away to Phoenix five days ago.

"At least Kyle got us a backup." She flipped some pages on her tablet. "Terry and Adriana have been delightful, though a few people are disappointed they aren't meeting your boyfriend."

I nodded, and she fixed an understanding look on me. The past few days hadn't gone well. Between Kyle leaving so quickly, the board asserting more oversight over this summit, and the intensity of the FBI/MC3 investigation, nothing was status quo. Kyle'd been great about listening to me, and it helped a bit in the moment. Thank God, he wasn't someone who just advised calming down

It had seemed like he'd make it. But that wasn't happening.

"You going to be okay? You look a little gray, and I don't think it's the lighting." Her on-going look of concern only made me feel worse since we had a room full of people to dazzle.

Kyle had melted down when he found out he wouldn't be able to leave when he'd planned because of last-minute press commitments. I knew it ate away at him. He'd been excited to talk about after-school programs helping him as a kid and now enjoying the work he did with them. Tamara hadn't supported this aspect of the program, but our sales team had liked the idea of bringing in a sports person to break up some of the business talk. It all tied to how kids in after school programs would make up the leaders and innovators of the future.

We had a small silent auction running too that included items from the major Detroit sports teams. Kyle had sent a package of Phoenix items as well. The proceeds would all go towards the foundation.

"Let's get the program started," Tamara said. "We need to leave as much time for one-on-ones as possible."

I nodded and shoved my confident businessman facade front and center. "Agreed. Wish me luck."

She nodded and pasted on a smile just like I did. "You got this. Just like always."

She returned to her table where she hosted a group from Chevy.

I headed for the stage and appreciated the bottles of water I spied next to the podium. My throat had gone dry talking to Tamara, so I needed some of that.

After a drink, I flipped on the mic, and I found my *everything's great* voice to address the audience. "Welcome, everyone. We're so glad you could join us tonight as part of our innovation summit. You've already heard a lot from us on what we're working on, and now I'd like to introduce you to Terry Kennedy, captain of the Detroit Arsenal. He was kind enough to fill in for our planned guest..."

---

Terry's presentation was great, of course.

But I missed Kyle so hard I ached. He'd texted that they'd hit traffic, and I'd replied with a picture of Terry at the podium and told him things were going fine. The evening needed to end though. My facade wouldn't last much longer even as I worked to prop it up.

Thankfully, the event entered the winding down phase. A few clusters of people talked. I chatted with Chaz Starling, our very first client and someone who'd become a friend over the years. Thankfully, I could relax since I had a solid relationship with him and the company he worked for.

"I'm so sorry. I've missed the entire thing." It took all I had to not dissolve as Kyle put his hand on my lower back. The simple touch meant everything. "Everything conspired against me. Hello, I'm Kyle Pressgrove." Kyle extended his hand.

"Pleasure to meet you," Chaz said as they shook. "I'd hoped I could meet the man who finally turned Austin's head. Thank you for arranging some of the great auction items. I came away with Kennedy's jersey. My daughter's a fan, and she's going to flip getting it for her birthday. She wants to be the first woman captain in the NHL. She's gunning for Team USA in the meantime."

"Good for her. Who does she play for now?"

"She's leading the points this season at Northwestern."

"Congratulations. That's a great school and a great program."

Chaz looked at his watch and shifted. "It's been a great evening, Austin. You unveiled some good stuff here. I've got an early meeting so I should get going. I'll see you at your office in the afternoon. You can be sure, though, that Kia is still with you." He shook my hand and then did the same with Kyle. "Really excellent meeting you."

"A pleasure," Kyle said.

"Have a good evening." I smiled and hoped it came off as genuine. Exhaustion rose up faster than I'd imagined possible. With Kyle next to me, I allowed the shields I had up all evening to fall away.

Four others remained who weren't on staff and they talked with Tamara. Their conversation appeared to be going well as they shared a laugh.

"Austin, I'm so sorry." He spoke softly, his earlier confidence cracked along with his voice. "It all went wrong."

"It's okay. I think everything turned out fine." He flinched for some reason as I took his hand, but then he squeezed back. Why did he do that? "I should join that conversation to finish this up. You can join me if you want."

I didn't let his hand go, and I couldn't miss the storm raging in his eyes. He was more upset than I'd imagined.

"Let's do this." Confident Kyle was back in place. He

had the same ability to do that as I did, except I rarely saw his resolve slip.

As we got to the group, they'd finished saying good night to Tamara. Quick introductions and more farewells followed.

"Well, I think we're done for the night." Tamara sounded relieved, and I couldn't blame her. "Kyle, you missed a good night. We raised just under ten thousand dollars for the foundation, and you helped make that happen. Thank you for helping get Terry here. The business conversations were mixed, but we'll see how most of that sorts out in tomorrow's individual meetings. Kyle, good to see you as always. Austin, I'll see you in the morning for our triage on how we'll handle the day."

"Good night, Tamara," we said at the same time. My heart fluttered—so much a couple thing, saying it together.

Alone with just the cleanup staff, Kyle slumped in a way I'd never seen. "I'm so sorry. This was important and I failed. I don't—" His voice cracked and he stopped. Running his hand through his hair and over his eyes, I thought for a moment he might cry. "I promise I tried... I..."

"It's okay. Terry did great, I promise." What was happening? He had no reason to be this upset. "The rest of the night went as good as it could have given everything."

"But that's just it..." I took a half step back at his increased volume, which he immediately modulated. "I should've been here for you... and for the speech... but really for you."

I was out of my depth. Kyle trembled with so many emotions. He wouldn't let me touch him though, keeping himself just out of reach. "You did the best you could, and you got someone to fill in for you. I couldn't have asked for more given..."

"But you shouldn't have had to. How many more times am I going to fail you because I'm in Phoenix?"

"Let's go talk about this. I'm sure—"

He shook his head. "I'm gonna go. I need... You need to focus on your meetings for tomorrow and making sure your company is okay, and not how I'm doing. I'll text you tomorrow."

His flight out was at six. No way we'd get time together. Did I push him to stay with me tonight like we were going to, or let him go?

"No." My voice cracked now. "Stay. Let's—"

I couldn't let this happen. Taking two quick steps forward, I pulled Kyle into me, and his shudders rocked me to my core.

"I'm sorry." He said it over and over, softer each time.

"Let's go home," I said. I already had all I needed, so I didn't need to leave Kyle for even a second. As we talked toward the ballroom entrance, I spotted his luggage against the wall. I kept Kyle's hand in mine as we walked, and I grabbed his bag as we left.

We didn't talk. I wanted to. There was a lot not being said, but I didn't want to force it either since I'd never seen Kyle like this. Where had all of this come from? From the moment he got traded, I told him he didn't have to do tonight because there was so much going on. Even when he'd asked Terry yesterday to be ready to fill in, he hadn't expressed this level of upset.

He remained silent on the way to my place, though he let me hold his hand as much as I could while driving.

"Do you want some food or anything?" I asked once we were inside.

He shook his head. "Let's just go to bed."

Whatever he wanted. "Okay."

We undressed and climbed into bed. This time, though, I wrapped my arm around him and pulled him tight. He took my hand in both of his and clutched it to his chest.

He didn't talk, and I didn't force it. Instead, I nuzzled the back of his head and occasionally kissed his neck. "It's going to be fine."

It wasn't.

When the alarm went off, he wasn't there.

On the desk in the living room was a note. *I'm sorry* was all it said.

Fuck.

# TWENTY-NINE

## KYLE

"What the hell is wrong with you? You haven't said anything to him since you left a note a week ago?" G asked, raising his voice.

I did to Austin exactly what he'd done to me—ghosted him when I shouldn't have. "I don't know what to do. The longer it goes, the worst it is, but I was terrible to him. At least he stopped texting a couple days ago."

We sat across from each other at Denny's. This was our hang out place since forever. Practice and Denny's. Game and Denny's. Sneaking out of the house once I could drive and Denny's. We still did it after games anytime we could.

Tonight, G was in Phoenix and had the overnight here. We kind of stood out since we wore suits. A couple of people recognized him—that magazine fame—when we came in and had gotten his autograph.

Garrett shook his head. "I don't even know what to say. You of all people aren't someone who does this."

I grunted.

"Is that the best you've got?"

"It's all I've got. Mom, Bobby, and you—all have given

variations of the same lecture. I'm not cut out to do this—at least not right now."

"Bullshit."

G got that right.

I didn't know how to fix my colossal fuck up. It impacted everything.

I wanted to call. To apologize. To find out how he was doing and how the company was doing.

It impacted my game too, which is not what my new team deserved. My last two games sucked—riddled with errors. Luckily, I'd only cost us a single goal, but I hadn't contributed any. If I'd been the coach, I'd have benched me. Of course it wouldn't look good to bench the highly touted new arrival.

My phone vibrated in my pocket. It wasn't anyone I knew, so I let it go.

"Next time I'm home, I'll try to see him. At least end things better than we did. I owe him that. In two weeks, I've got a stretch of off days and I'll be home, so we can talk face-to-face."

"You can't let this sit. It's only going to make you crazy."

The phone rang again. Who was calling so late? I pulled the phone and saw a Detroit number I didn't recognize. G and I traded shrugs, and I swiped to answer.

"Hello?"

"Is this Kyle Pressgrove?"

"Yes. Who's this, please?"

G shot me a questioning look, and I shook my head.

"This is Officer Morales with the Detroit Police Department. You're in Greta Pressgrove's phone as the emergency contact. She was in a car accident this evening and has been taken to Henry Ford Hospital."

The world spun. I might as well have been slammed into the boards by a hulking defenseman.

I dropped the phone, and it skittered across the table, narrowly missing my plate of food.

"Kyle?" I couldn't focus on G.

I fumbled for the phone but gripped it on my second try.

"How... Is she..."

"What is it?" G's concern mixed with impatience pierced my focus, and I mouthed "Mom" in response.

"Paramedics on scene reported she was unconscious and had a broken arm. I don't have more information, but I am en route to the hospital. Are you able to get there?"

"I..." I looked to G, my brain locked up.

G reached over and took the phone. "Hi. This is Garrett Howell. I'm a friend of Kyle's. Who am I speaking to, please?"

My mind flashed back to when the call had come about Dad. We'd been home from school about a half hour and...

"He's in Phoenix, so it'll take some time to get him there." He listened more but kept his eyes trained on me. "Can he use the number you called from to reach you?"

I was hours away from her. Bobby was even farther because he and Seb had gone to Vancouver for a working vacation. The Arsenal were out of town too.

"One of us will be in touch with his travel plans. Please let us know if you get more information in the meantime." Another pause. "Thank you, Officer Morales."

Uncontrollable shakes racked me.

Mom had to be okay.

"I gotta call Bobby and let him know."

G nodded as he passed the phone back. As I reached, he grabbed my hand as he put the phone in it. Grasping me tight with both of his hands, he held my gaze with a look of determination that helped pull me back.

"She *will* be okay." He said it with such conviction I couldn't imagine the universe going against him. "Call Bobby and I'll get us paid up. Then we'll figure out how to get you home."

Bobby's phone went to voicemail, which wasn't a surprise given the time. I hated leaving this news in a message, but I couldn't risk that he'd try to call me back while I was on a plane. I got in touch with Quinn, who worked in the team's front office. They said they'd make the right notifications in the morning and to let them know if there was anything they or anyone on the team could do.

My mind raced, sorting out options on what to do. There were direct flights to Detroit. But even if there was still one this late, it would take almost four hours. Mom needed someone there when she woke up.

"Could you see what my flight options are?" I asked as we got in the car.

"On it."

Who could I call in Detroit that I was close enough to who could check on her? The options were limited with the team on the road. I didn't have contact information in my phone for any of her friends. As I drove, determined to not speed too much, I returned over and over to the one person who seemed like the best and worst option. I keyed the phone button on the steering wheel and spoke. "Call Austin."

From the corner of my eye, I saw G's surprise. Yeah, I couldn't believe it either. Austin had no reason to pick up. As his phone rang on the car's speakers, G looked up from his screen.

"The last flights out are boarding right now. After

midnight, there's nothing. The first direct is at six. Probably your best choice since connections would just add time."

Fuck. I wasn't surprised, but still, that was hours away. Maybe I could get a charter. How did I even do that? The team used one sometimes. Maybe Quinn could help? I'd pay whatever.

"You've reached Austin Murray. I can't take your call right now. Please..."

He always answered the phone... Unless he blocked or ignored me... Or actually ignores his phone sometimes now.

I hit another button so I could speak a text message. "It's an emergency. Please call if you're in Detroit." I clicked again and told the car to send it to Austin.

"Do you think he will?" G asked

I wished I felt more confident. "Knowing that it's an emergency should—"

The phone ring filled the car as the center screen lit up with his name. I punched the accept button.

"Austin, thank God."

"Kyle, what's wrong?" He sounded sleepy, concerned but thankfully not angry.

"It's my mom." My voice broke.

G rested his hand on my thigh, a comforting touch.

"Tell me."

I laid out the situation. "Can you... I'm sorry, I know I shouldn't ask this, but could you go to the hospital and be there if she wakes up or anything? She at least knows you. I'm not sure I can get there until almost noon tomorrow."

I heard rustling like he was moving the sheets. I pictured him in his boxers, hair tussled. He'd be moving in his determined, *I've got something to do* mode. "Of course. I'll go to the hospital and be there for her. I can also get you a flight tonight. It might take an hour to sort out but—"

"Really? That'd be amazing. I'll pay whatever."

"Let's just get you here first."

I released my death grip on the steering wheel. With so many things to worry about, at least getting home sooner than later would happen. G offered a small smile and nodded.

"Thank you. I'm on my way to my place to pack a bag."

"Did you get to go out with Garrett?"

Did he watch the game or just keep up with the schedule? "Yeah. We were grabbing a bite when DPD called."

"I'm glad you weren't alone when that call came in."

The call was headed into awkward territory. Did he miss me like I missed him?

Luckily, I pulled into the parking lot of my apartment building, so we wouldn't have to drag this out. "I just parked. Let me go get packed so I'm ready to go when you have the details."

"Sounds good. I'll call you back as soon as possible."

"Thank you, Austin. I appreciate this more than you know."

He softly said, "Greta's important. You need to get here for her. I'm glad I can help."

He disconnected, and I turned off the car. G opened his door, but I didn't move.

"Okay?" he asked.

"No. Did you hear how he sounded? He didn't care this would keep him up for hours. He had something to take care of and he did it."

"He had something to take care of *for you.*" G looked at me. The concern bouncing through his eyes didn't help the conflict raging inside me. "I don't know Austin that well, but I don't think he'd have moved like that for just anyone.

And *you* knew you could call him. Maybe you two can talk while you're home."

He stared at me to the point it got uncomfortable.

"Maybe." I finally got out and headed inside. "One thing at a time."

# THIRTY

## AUSTIN

Four hours after we spoke, I still couldn't believe Kyle had called. I'd almost drifted off when the phone rang, and I'd fumbled to grab it off the nightstand. When I saw the missed call had come from Kyle, I'd figured he'd butt dialed. Then the text arrived, and of course I called.

Not a day went by without me almost calling. I didn't know what to say to him though. If it'd been anger at me, I could've apologized, but how did I fix it when he beat himself up over a perceived problem.

The possibility of saying the wrong thing was too high.

So I did nothing.

I kept my focus on AMDD. Since the innovation summit, Tamara, me, and the staff continued the task of damage control from the Atlas problem. The FBI traced the breach back to a group in China, along with over one hundred similar hacks that had happened in the same week. While a new advisory was issued to help companies prevent future intrusions, Atlas wasn't satisfied. We expected a suit from them any day now.

Tamara and I had a board meeting on our calendars for

this morning. We'd spoken to them every day to provide updates and discuss plans. They weren't usually this hands-on, but between the financial forecast that already troubled them and the hack, they had a vested interest in getting details. Frankly, a vote of no confidence against me wouldn't be a surprise at this point.

As I sat in the intensive care waiting room—I'd been directed here from the emergency room—in case there were any updates, I reviewed what I'd prepared for the meeting.

"Mr. Murray?"

I looked up at the nurse in the doorway. "Yes?"

She came over and took a seat next to me. "Good morning. I'm Linda Montgomery, the charge nurse here. I have an update for you. Mrs. Pressgrove is stable. We performed emergency surgery for some internal bleeding in her abdomen and that was successful. Her broken arm has also been set. The MRI showed no other concerns. As soon as she's released from surgical recovery, she'll be sent down here. We've got a room ready for her."

"Thank you. I'll let her son know. He should be here within the next hour or so."

"Good. Glad he was able to get here so quickly, especially since he played last night."

I found it comforting that at least one of the nurses taking care of Greta knew who her son was. Logically, it didn't matter, but it still seemed good.

"Luckily, we got it worked out." I smiled.

She nodded and stood. "I'll let you know once she's settled here."

"Thanks again. I'll be here if anything comes up."

She left the room after a quick smile at me. I texted the update to Kyle.

*Surgery. Jesus. Okay. Stable is good though, right?*

I typed back immediately. I didn't want him worrying over a delayed response. *Stable is very good. The nurse was very confident sounding when she brought the info.*

The three dots appeared so quickly I thought he must've started typing before he finished reading.

*I was just told we'll be on the ground in less than thirty minutes. Hopefully I can be there by the time she wakes up.*

I smiled at the thought. *She'll like that. I'll double check with the car service that they're monitoring the flight and know your arrival status. I want to make sure they get you here as fast as possible.*

His next message took a minute. He typed, stopped, typed some more, and repeated that cycle a few times.

The wait flared the butterflies in my chest.

I stopped looking until it vibrated.

*Thank you for all of this. You made this much easier even though you didn't have to. I'll let you know when I get in the car.*

I didn't need to think about my response. *You're welcome. See you soon.*

Not even dots this time.

I'd hoped—selfishly—that he would have said something about looking forward to seeing me. Why would I think that? He was here to see his mom, the family that means so much to him. When we talked last night, I'd heard the hesitation through the fear in his voice. He hadn't wanted to talk to me, but he'd reached out anyway.

The back and forth of *could we, should we* had to end.

He'd reached out to a friend. With Detroit on the road, of course I'd be someone he'd call. Plus I liked Greta, so that made it all the easier.

I reasoned myself around and around. It didn't help.

Kyle and I were done.

I knew it when he left that note.

I'd become more sure of it when neither of us even said "hello," like he'd done when I'd ghosted him. I should've taken the chance...

I sighed and rubbed at my tired eyes.

Maybe we'd salvage a friendship, though it'd be difficult because I knew how good it felt to love him. The warmth in my chest. The goose bumps at the slightest touch. The desire to be near him.

Just the thought quickened my pulse. He'd be standing in front of me in less than an hour.

I already wanted to wrap him in my arms and comfort him.

Selfishly, that same hug would give me some of his energy, which always managed to calm me. It'd be ideal to soak up some of that before the board meeting.

"Mr. Murray?" Nurse Montgomery startled me. I'd zoned out more than I thought I had.

"Yes? Is everything okay?"

"Yes. We've got Mrs. Pressgrove settled. She's resting, vital signs are good, and she's been awake a few times, and they removed the ventilator before they brought her down. You can come back and see her if you'd like."

Wow. Time flew. I looked at my watch—sure enough it'd been nearly thirty minutes since I'd talked to her.

Should I do that? She barely knew me. On the other hand, it might help her to know that someone was here.

"Sure. Then I can give a first-hand report back."

"Follow me."

I closed my laptop and left it and my backpack behind. I doubted the few people here were going to take my things from a waiting room. I did pick up my phone just in case Kyle reached out.

Going through the double doors that Nurse Montgomery had to swipe to open, it hit me that I'd not spent time in hospitals. I'd never had to be in one, and so far, my parents had lived healthy lives too. The beeps from so many machines from the individual patient bays were disconcerting. On the other hand, I took comfort from the central area where the nurses worked so they could see all the patients and also see if anyone was at the front needing assistance. My designer brain couldn't help but be impressed at how much thought went into the function.

In bed, covered by a blanket, Greta looked small and fragile—far from the vibrant woman I'd met. Her face showed signs of the airbag impact with some bruises.

"I can let you have five minutes." She left me before I could even say thank you.

I stood at the foot of the bed, deciding if I should move closer.

Finally, I moved next to her. I debated touching her, maybe on her shoulder since I couldn't see her hands.

That seemed too familiar.

Instead, I just spoke quietly. "Hi, Greta. It's Austin. Kyle introduced us." That sounded ridiculous. "He'll be here soon."

She didn't react, but hopefully she heard.

My phone vibrated. Did Kyle somehow know I was back here?

I glanced at the message on the lock screen. *I just got in the car so I'll be there soon.*

"Very soon," I said and smiled to myself.

I left her side to talk with Nurse Montgomery. "I just heard from Kyle. He's in a car on the way, should be about thirty minutes."

"Perfect. I'll let the doctor know so that he can stop by close to that time and give him the complete update."

"I know he'll appreciate that. Thank you."

She went back to her computer screen, and I went back to the waiting room.

I texted Kyle to let him know that his Mom was back from recovery and that they'd be ready to give him a full update.

*Great. Thanks.*

I studied the reply for longer than I should've. I'd hoped for a "see you soon" or something to that effect.

# THIRTY-ONE

## KYLE

As soon as the elevator door opened, I saw Austin. He sat hunched over his laptop and looked as rumpled as I felt—his hair was askew, and he wore jeans and a sweatshirt.

The ding of the elevator got his attention. Our eyes locked and he stood.

Wheeling my bag behind me, I went to him, and as soon as we were close enough, he pulled me into an embrace. I needed the hug, but I'd expected to have to initiate it. But he grabbed me, stepped in, and gave me the tight, comforting touch I needed.

The small bit of resolve I'd held on to crumbed, and I cried. He held tight, a rock keeping me upright and stable as I unleashed all the pent-up emotions I'd carried since I'd seen him last.

I missed this—feeling him, being near him. All of it.

And I'd walked away from it.

"Kyle, the nurse is here," Austin said as he patted me on the back.

I worked to quickly compose myself before I let him go.

He gave me an extra squeeze across my lower back before he let me step back and turn.

"Nurse Montgomery, this is Kyle,"

The kindness in her eyes reminded me of Mom, and it almost triggered another emotional outburst. I took a couple of deep breaths to hold that back.

"I'm sorry to be meeting you under these circumstances. The good news is your mom is resting comfortably, and the surgery was successful. The doctor will be here in a few minutes to tell you more. I can take you back to see her if you'd like."

"Yes, please. Thank you." I turned back to Austin. "Thank you for being here. Helping me to get here."

He nodded, but I couldn't fully read his expression. Was he as confused as I was by all this?

"I should..." So many responses collided in my head, I couldn't pick one fast enough.

"You need get back there." Austin's tone was solemn, and he looked down at the floor for a brief moment. "I've got an early meeting with Tamara, so I'm going to head home and get showered."

I nodded, appreciating he laid out a plan. It'd be great if he'd stay here, but I couldn't ask that after all he'd already done.

"If you need anything, call. Okay?"

All I managed was a nod before I gave him another quick hug. "Thank you so much."

I almost told him I loved him, but he probably didn't want to hear that, and more importantly this wasn't the time.

"Anytime," he said.

We released each other, and I went to the nurse with my luggage in tow. Before I went through the doors, I stole one look back to find Austin's gaze still on me. Thankfully, the door closed automatically so I couldn't just run back to the safety of his embrace.

---

I DIDN'T HAVE much experience with hospitals. I'd been to the emergency room three times as a kid because of a broken arm and two sprained ankles. For those, I was in and out in a few hours. I'd been next to Mom's bed for what felt like an entirety.

Nothing changed. She laid there looking peaceful. Machines around her beeped. The bruises on her face made it look like she'd been in a fight. I'd never seen her looking this broken.

Sitting next to her—my hand on top of hers so she could know I'm here—I was a mess, replaying the moments with Austin I'd had. That last look... did he want to say something? Should I have spilled out an apology? I'm sure I handled the whole thing wrong as I had the other night. Other than G, I hadn't told anyone what had happened. I couldn't face telling either Bobby or Mom. Besides, I already knew what they'd tell me.

Mom's hand flexed under mine—at least I think it did.

"Mom? I'm here. Bobby's on the way too."

Another flex. No mistake this time.

"Shouldn't you..." Her eyes fluttered open, and it looked like she was trying to focus on the room. Her hand tightened into a vice.

"Mom?" She turned to my voice. Her eyes still didn't seem to fully focus, but her mouth curved into a very slight smile. "Hey, Mom. It's so good to see you awake."

"Kyle?" Her voice sounded rough, dry, and raspy. "I'm

so sorry."

"You got nothing to be sorry about. Everything is gonna be okay."

"I have not..." She tried to clear her throat. "Water? Can I? Is there some?"

I didn't see any, and I was sure I couldn't give her the coffee I had with me. I probably needed permission to give her anything and let them know she was awake.

I clicked the call button that lay on the bed next to her hand.

"Yes? May I help you?" Nurse Montgomery's voice came back.

"Hi. Yes. My mom is waking up. She's asking for water."

"That's great." She sounded very pleased. I'd liked the nurse from the moment I'd met her. She had a cool, calm demeanor even with all the critical patients around her. "I'll be right there after I call the doctor."

"I hope she brings water," Mom sputtered out. "Is it still Wednesday?"

"No. It's Thursday morning."

"How are you here? You had a game. What about practice today?"

I couldn't help but chuckle as she tried to admonish me, which came out weird with her dry voice. "I'm here because somebody decided to ram into your car last night."

Nurse Montgomery and Doctor Snow came in. The nurse had water and went to the opposite side of the bed, and mom turned to her to get to the straw.

"Mrs. Pressgrove, it's good to see you awake. Kyle, can you please step out for a moment while we do some examinations? You can wait by the nurse's station because this won't take long. Then we can talk about the test results I got a few minutes ago."

"Of course."

I leaned against the nurse's station, letting it hold me up. Relief rushed through me. Mixed with the extreme tired, it verged on more than I could deal with.

"Are you okay?"

I turned and found another of the nurses looking at me. "Yes. Sorry. Just wiped out by it all, you know."

"I understand." He had a kind smile—I imagined all nurses had that—as he got up from his chair and took a tablet into one of the other patient areas.

I pulled out my phone and texted Bobby to give me something to do. I couldn't fall apart when Mom needed me, so it all needed to stay bottled up.

*She's awake! And already giving me grief because I'm missing practice. The doc is with her now. I'll let you know when I know more.*

He'd be in flight or near it, so I didn't expect an immediate reply for him.

My finger hovered over Austin's name as I debated whether to call or text.

I clicked call.

It went directly to voicemail. "You've reached Austin Murray. I can't take your call right now. Please leave a message and I'll get back to you as soon as possible."

"Hi. Wanted to let you know Mom's awake, and the doctor is with her. I thought you'd like to know." What should I say? Too much silence here would be weird. "Thank you for your help last night. I hope your meetings are going okay."

I disconnected so I wouldn't leave more awkward dead air.

Before I pocketed my phone, it lit up with texts. My Arsenal teammates had just heard the news and all kinds of well wishes and offers of help rolled in. As I read, a call from Kennedy came in.

"Hey, KP." Kennedy's concerned voice sounded loud and clear. "We got the news this morning about Greta. Is she okay? Are you on the way? How can we help?"

Wow. These guys. Right there to help. I blinked back tears.

"I got here a few hours ago, and she's just woken up. She's banged up, but the prognosis is good."

"That's good, man. We're all thinking about her. If you need anything, let us know. I'll call Adriana in a second and let her know. I'm sure she'd be okay if you called her too."

"I appreciate that." My voice wavered but didn't crack.

This team always rallied. Anytime a player or a player's family went through something, they didn't do it alone.

Nurse Montgomery appeared at my side, and I took the phone from my ear. "Doctor Snow is ready to give an update as soon as you're done."

"Sorry, Kennedy. The doc's ready. I need to go."

"Got it. We're getting on a plane in a few minutes, but you can text me."

"Thanks again. And thank the guys for me too. You all almost blew up my phone with all the messages, and I appreciate that. Talk to you later."

I entered Mom's space, braced—or trying to be—for whatever the doctor had to say. Mom looked tired but more alert now. I went to the bedside and kissed her forehead before I turned my attention to the doctor.

"Things are looking quite good. The fact that she's awake and becoming more alert is very encouraging. We're going to send her for a new MRI, and I expect to see improvements. We'll continue to monitor for any concussion symptoms. We had to repair some internal bleeding in the abdomen. That will keep her in the hospital for two or three days more. As she heals, she'll probably need help for a time even once she's back home. Of course, things can change. I want to caution about that. But right now, everything is looking good for a fairly rapid recovery."

"Thank God." I looked down to her. "I had no idea when I moved you'd go to such elaborate measures to get me to come home."

"Just one of the tricks in the Mom Handbook." She rolled her eyes at me. Her humor returning in full force told me even more than what the doctor said.

"I'll check back when I've got the new test results. The team here can reach me anytime if needed. If the next twenty-four hours go well, we'll move to a private room on a general floor. For now, just rest."

"Thank you, doctor," she said as she and the nurse left.

I sat in the chair, relieved but not fully relaxed.

"I hate that you came all the way up here, but thank you."

"Like I would do anything else. You're important. Besides, you were always with me when I broke something."

"You never did it in such a spectacular fashion as I just did."

We shared a smile, and I shook my head. "Well, I don't know that any of us needed this drama, so maybe don't do it again."

This crisis seemed mostly passed. Once Bobby got here, we'd figure out the plan for making sure she had help until the doc said she was fully recovered.

Meanwhile, her busy life kicked in as she gave me a list of things to do and people to call to let them know what had happened. I was glad she felt good enough to ask for such things, and I'd happily do everything she listed.

# THIRTY-TWO

## AUSTIN

Barely controlled chaos.

That summed up the day.

Helping Kyle and Greta turned into the only good thing that occurred.

Atlas had made their demands this morning—the only way for AMDD to not be sued was to fire Tamara, Max, and me. Knowing this before the board meeting allowed us to make a plan. I had no problem sacrificing myself and we couldn't make a case strong enough to save Max. We did plead that Tamara should stay because to terminate the leads of both the technical and business sides would doom the company.

I convinced Tamara that I was the better one to go. We had enough to talent to carry on the design and tech. Atlas agreed so the board and Tamara voted yes to the changes.

My tenure was done—effective immediately.

For better or worse on my way home, I decided to return to the hospital. When I tried to return Kyle's call, it went to voicemail. I couldn't be sure if he ignored me, couldn't get a signal where he was, if something else had happened, or maybe he was getting needed sleep.

At the ICU desk, I asked if I could see Greta, and the guy there got up to see if she'd see me. After a moment, Bobby came out of Greta's space. He exited through the security doors and offered a handshake as he reached me.

"Hi, Austin. Thanks for getting Kyle here so quickly." He looked and sounded exhausted.

"I'm glad I could help. How's Greta? I'd heard that she woke up."

He nodded and directed us away from the doors but not fully into the waiting room. "Things look pretty good. She's mostly sleeping. When she's awake, she's frustrated that she's stuck in bed and brought us all here." He chuckled and I smiled. I liked that he could laugh a little. "I managed to send Kyle home. I got here about an hour ago, and he was dead on his feet. Looks like you could use some rest too? I heard you were here for a while."

"It's been..." I sighed. "A day."

"You want to grab a cup of coffee? I could use some, and Mom's dozed off again."

I wasn't sure how this would go, but my curiosity was piqued. Bobby asked me to stay put while he went back to the desk to tell them how to reach him if needed.

"Luckily, the gift shop has a Starbucks in it."

"Sadly, that was closed last night. You'd think they'd be able to make better coffee from a vending machine, but that wasn't the case in the E.R. or up here."

Maybe that could be my new career—good vending coffee.

"Well, we owe you at least one coffee, so I can start to make good on that." He smiled. He didn't seem anything other than tired.

We walked in silence, and the guy seemed pretty chill. Bobby was a therapist, so he probably didn't come out yelling at people even if he was pissed off.

After we got the coffee, we found an open table.

"Kyle hasn't mentioned you two since he moved. I know the relocation hasn't been easy on him, but are you two okay?"

My mouth dropped open before I could catch it. Kyle hadn't told Bobby what happened? I'd thought he was an open book with his family.

I couldn't school my body language fast enough as I slumped back in the chair and let out a sigh.

He wasted no time diving in. I guessed the small talk happened back in the waiting room. "I've never seen him happier than when things were going right between you two. He holds very tight to the words that got dropped into his head—for better or worse—by some of our extended family. Mom and I have tried for years, but can't quite get him to let go. You can imagine that what happened last night hits a lot of his worst fears."

I nodded and repositioned myself to sit forward at the table. To give my hands something to do, I wrapped them around the coffee cup. "Yeah, he told me about that. It's one of the reasons I jumped to help." I tried to meet Bobby's gaze and not drift somewhere that would be easier. "I know how hard it was for him when he couldn't get here for the presentation he was supposed to do too. I shouldn't have let him withdraw after that, but... I'm way out of my comfort zone with relationship stuff."

"Can I offer some unsolicited advice?"

"Please." If anyone knew how to possibly fix what I'd done to Kyle, Bobby would. The business was fucked but maybe I could find a way to keep Kyle in my life. "Make him hear you. He can be very stubborn when it comes to beating himself up, so you'll have to be forceful to make him understand that he's being, frankly, a dumbass."

He chuckled at the word, and that brought a slight smile to my lips. It was the funniest thing I'd heard all day, and I imagined this was a long-running term between brothers.

I looked into my coffee and took a sip as I considered.

Maybe this could be saved.

I ran my hand through my hair. Stress, anger, and sadness combined in the center of my chest. I thought I might simply fly apart.

"I think we could really make something amazing between us. The love and calm I get from him is incredible. I think I give some of that back to him. I need to figure out my next move with him and, well, everything."

"Should I ask? You said it'd been a day."

"I'm not sure you should be burdened..." I paused a minute and then blurted everything out. "I lost my company today. Some things happened. Now that I don't have a job, I can re-evaluate a lot of stuff."

Bobby nodded and groaned. "Oh man, I'm sorry. Is there anything—"

"No. Actually I'm strangely pretty good." I didn't look forward to telling my parents what I'd allowed to happen, but otherwise I truly did feel okay about how things had played out. I wanted to chart a different course.

"Fair enough. If you change your mind, don't hesitate to ask." His laser focus on me said that he meant it too. "I'll shift back to what we started with. Kyle would probably check me into the nearest wall if he knew I was giving advice on him, but I don't want him wondering later *what if*. Since I'm not sure he'll get off his ass and make the first move, maybe you will."

"How long's he in town for?"

"He's wants to rejoin the team when they're here next Friday. He's off tonight anyway, so he'll talk to the team tomorrow after we get an update. Mom's already told him that he should go back. I'm able to stay for several weeks. It's not ideal, but I can work with most of my clients over video-conference for a short time. And Seb's on board."

"I suppose the worst that can happen is our next talk becomes an official end." I took a long drink of the coffee, draining it.

Bobby offered a shrug. "I suppose so." He downed his coffee. "Let's head back up. I know Mom would love to see you. She likes you, a lot. I've heard about the nice guy who did the dishes. Way to make me and Seb look bad." He raised his eyebrows at me as he smirked.

I couldn't resist a chuckle. "Sorry. I'll keep that in mind next time I'm there." We stood and went toward the elevators. "Thank you, for the talk and the coffee."

Bobby had gone above and beyond. It was good to talk about Kyle with someone who knew him. With the turmoil at AMDD, Tamara and I had been preoccupied, and we hadn't talked much about personal stuff recently.

Bobby gave me some food for thought, even though I didn't quite know how to execute on it.

# THIRTY-THREE

## KYLE

"You ready to go out as the enemy?" Owen, Phoenix's captain, stepped up next to me as we waited to go out. It was the first time I'd be going out on this ice as the opponent.

"It's weird."

I didn't want to go into how much I truly hated it.

On the other hand, it had worked out perfectly that team management had let me come back while we were here. I got the time at home I desperately wanted to make sure Mom got back home okay. I got to go to one last checkup and heard firsthand how well she was healing. She still had bruises, some that rivaled the ugliness of pucks slamming into me in an unpadded area.

I'd said my goodbyes before coming to the rink since we were flying after tonight's game to be in New York for tomorrow.

The intro played and the fans roared. I knew the reel well—I'd been in it until recently.

"Is your mom here to see you go over to the dark side?"

"No. My brother and I convinced her home was the place to watch. It wasn't easy, but she relented."

"Maybe she'll come down to catch a game before the end of the season. I'd love to meet her." Owen did a great job as captain. He'd made me and the other guys feel welcome. He'd checked in daily while I was home with Mom too.

Kennedy had been a great captain. Owen was different, but I already liked his way with the team. His enthusiasm for the game matched mine, and that really helped me focus as I made the move. He kept me out of my head.

We charged out of the tunnel as we got our signal to go, the intro still finishing out and all the lights flashing through the crowd. I saw my teammates—former teammates—on the other side of the ice. I'd hung out with them a little bit earlier. We had practice before they did, and I'd hung back to talk for a few minutes. Several of them I'd seen over the past week as they'd checked on Mom.

"Please welcome back to Arsenal ice, three former players: Kyle Pressgrove, Nicolas Helson, and Troy Feldman. It's great to have you back, but don't look for any mercy tonight."

Damn, that was nice. The crowd got extra noisy, and that meant even more.

Sawyer Herron, my left wing, skated alongside as I finished up a half lap, waving at people who waved at me from the stands. "I wonder if they'll be so happy if you score on them tonight."

I laughed. "Hopefully, we'll find out."

I headed to the bench and looked up at the scoreboard to check the time, and the logo for Austin's company was gone. In its place was something called Digital Interface

Innovation. What had happened? Had he pulled out? I thought sponsorships went for the year.

The game was hard-fought and much closer than anticipated. Clearly Billington was a good pick up for the Arsenal. Defense seemed transformed. At the same time, Phoenix played stronger because the three of us had integrated into the team so quickly. This game was far different than when Detroit was in Phoenix before my trade.

A couple of times, the Arsenal got breakaways, and I had to hold back from cheering. It was a reflex to cheer for orange. Luckily, we shut those down.

We ended up down to what I hated—an overtime shootout. Coach planned to have me shoot second. I didn't want to do that here.

Detroit put Kennedy up for their second shooter, and I liked that even less.

Both first-round shooters made it.

Kennedy's shot got covered by our goalie.

I'd make a dent in this standoff if I scored.

I skated out to the center, and the crowd that had cheered me nearly three hours ago let loose a torrent of boos. I stole a look over to Herron and shrugged. He shrugged back and gave me thumbs up.

I looked down the ice at Lindsay. He'd had a good game —both goalies had.

As I stood at the dot and before the ref had the puck set, Lindsay raised his stick to me. I raised mine back. We knew each other's tricks so well, and I hadn't been gone long enough for either of us to forget or to have new moves.

The ref checked us both and blew his whistle.

The crowd got to their feet and booed louder. Of course they wanted me to fail. I'd feel the same way about an opposing shooter, but it stung nonetheless.

Skating down the ice, I focused on Lindsay while he studied me. This had to be just right. I came in and kept straight on target and made a last minute shift to my left. Lindsay didn't fall for that.

I expected he wouldn't.

What he left me though was a gap between his leg pad and blocker. I shot and the puck sailed in and hit the back of the net.

The red light and buzzer went off, setting off even more crowd noise.

As I turned at the boards to go back to the bench, I looked to Lindsay, and we traded head nods.

Crenshaw was up next for Detroit, and he made his goal, leaving us tied at two-two.

Owen took our third shot, and he wrapped up the game. Relief flooded me—not only did we win, but the shootout wasn't going to drag on.

As we cleared the ice, I was held back to be one of the three stars of the game, another surreal experience. I'd had this honor quite a few times as an Arsenal player, but to get it on the opposite side felt like I betrayed a friend.

The fans were appreciative even though I'd helped seal the loss for Detroit. I raised my stick in thanks.

David waited for me as I exited the ice. "Hey, man, Austin's here to see you."

What? Why?

"Um. Okay. Let me get cleaned up, and I'll come over. Thanks for letting me know."

I wanted to send Austin away, but it wasn't something I could ask David to do. It wouldn't be fair. I couldn't ignore him and just leave him waiting either because that would be a dick move. I owed him better anyway. He'd messaged a couple of times, and I'd said I was busy with

Mom. I didn't know what to say so I defaulted to saying nothing.

"I'll let him know." He clapped me on the shoulder.

Our locker room was jubilant, and several people took a moment to congratulate me on my solid game against my former home.

I had texts from Bobby and Mom—many texts. Despite the fact they watched together in her living room, they had a group chat between them and me. I'd have to read them later because their play-by-play looked hilarious.

*You need to know that Bobby is sitting here coaching because you keep letting Crenshaw get by on your left. The man always dekes and goes left... keep up with him!*

*Someone needs to coach him. He played with Crenshaw for four years. He should know better.*

They'd never done anything like that before—and I loved it. Maybe it'd become a thing. They wrapped up saying they had fun, congratulated me on the win, and wished me safe travels. I shot them a reply with hearts of all colors.

I got showered quick and into my suit. As I headed over to where Austin was, I stopped to let Lenny, our equipment manager, know where I'd gone. Despite the loss, the guys on the Detroit side offered up fist bumps and back slaps.

The Detroit waiting room had a couple of people in it, and I immediately recognized the back of Austin's head and the awkward way he stood watching the TV that played postgame coverage. He stood about as far away as he could get from the people talking with Kennedy.

My heart betrayed me as I drank in his slightly rumpled look—Detroit jersey over what had to be a layer or two of other clothes. My instinct was to bolt even as I felt pulled to him.

As the screen went black before a commercial, my reflection popped up. He turned and his face brightened as I came toward him. That only intensified the feels, sending goose bumps across me as he offered the smallest hint of a smile. This wasn't comfortable for him either.

"Austin. It's good to see you." At least my voice stayed even.

"I know it's not great to ambush you here, but..." He kept his voice low. "I miss you. I hate that I didn't pursue you after you snuck out but—" He sounded so earnest and a little bit broken. My defenses lowered even more. I held back from reaching out to him though. If we touched at all, I might shatter.

While he'd trailed off talking, he still held my gaze. Maybe he couldn't look away. I certainly had no choice but to stare into the gorgeous eyes that I'd missed.

"Please stop." Every emotion I had bubbled just under the surface and threatened to spill over. "I hate myself for doing that, and I'm sorry. I'm trying so hard to be a proper adult, and I keep fucking up."

"I think we've both fucked up a fair bit over the past few weeks. Let's reset. I'm"—he took in a huge breath, so big I saw his chest expand even with all the layers he wore—"moving to Phoenix. I want us to really give this a shot. I like how I feel when I'm around you. I like how we are together. If you're willing, let's prove we can be amazing together."

Damn.

Moving to Phoenix though? I never saw that coming.

All I could do was stare.

Many nights in the past week, I'd dreamed different aspects of our life together—from making pancakes again to the vacation we'd talked about to just waking up for a lazy morning together.

That's how much he was in me.

I had to say something. But what? My heart thumped loudly as it declared victory, leaving my brain scrambling to find words.

# THIRTY-FOUR

## AUSTIN

HE LOOKED SO GOOD. That suit... The slightly damp hair...

Had it really only been a couple weeks since we'd been together? It seemed like it could've been months or years since we'd spent that amazing day together.

Memories of the night at his place rushed back and made it hard to concentrate on what I was here to do.

I'd managed to get the first words out, but the longer it took him to reply, the more this looked like a horrible mistake.

"Moving to Phoenix? That's... That's huge. And you got a place already?" His mouth hung open. Had he lost his train of thought too? Maybe he'd gotten stuck like I did in the moment. "And... well... yes. I want to try. I've missed you. I've missed not being able to talk to you about stuff, talk to you about Mom, talk to you about being stuck in Phoenix."

He came closer and took my hand without hesitation.

"I should've just called... gotten over myself. But how are you relocating?" His brow furrowed again, deep lines running across his forehead and right above his nose. Damn cute creases too. I wanted to trace them, smooth them out. "Wait, did something happen? Something happened because I didn't show up. Oh, shit."

Kennedy's group was looking at us. He offered a slight smile and steered his group into the hallway, which was super nice since Kyle wasn't even on the team anymore.

"That's why your logo's not up there anymore. Shit. Shit. Shit. I'm so sorry."

I put a finger against his lips, which muffled more apologies. He bugged his eyes out.

"Long story short, AMDD isn't mine anymore." A week had past and even though it's what I wanted, it still stabbed at my heart every time I had to talk about it. I wouldn't sugarcoat it for Kyle; though why Bobby hadn't told him I wasn't sure. "Someone had to be sacrificed for what happened, and it was me."

He started to say something, and I shook my head.

"This isn't your fault. But you know what? It's the best thing that could've happened. I got bought out, which makes for a great nest egg—on top of the money I'd already been saving. You're starting over in Phoenix." I took a deep breath to quell the shot of anxiety in my chest. This was so against my norm. "I'm going to do the same. We can truly begin again. We can date and sort our stuff out."

He squeezed my hand, a bit tight for comfort, but I had no intention of moving it.

"I don't know what to say. Are you sure? I was a distraction that cost you... well, everything."

"After years of hearing there's more than work, you gave me a glimpse of what's possible and someone I wanted to figure that out with. I totally get that I may move and we may not work. It's important to know we gave it a fair shot though."

"I hope I'm worth it." He finally smiled broadly, and that pushed away some of my fears. I liked seeing some of his self-assuredness return. "What about your parents? Are you moving them?"

I laughed because that conversation had been ridiculously bad. The first thing they asked was if they needed to look for work. I assured them they were set up, and no one could take their money away. Still, they talked to me like I'd made a childish mistake. Kyle didn't need to know all of that just now.

"That would be a hard no. They're wildly disappointed. I'm not even sure they'll come visit. I'm keeping my place in Detroit, though, for visits."

Kyle's smile remained, and it warmed me. Thank God he liked the idea of the move. I'd imagined a version where he got angry instead—that one had sucked.

"I'm keeping mine too. Figure it'll be good for summers and a place to stay when I'm here so I don't have to crash with anyone else."

I almost suggested we could combine houses but held that back. Maybe in a few months we could talk about that.

"By the time you get back to Phoenix, I'll be there full-time. It'll take a few days to get my house fully set up, but it'll be good enough to start with."

Kyle chuckled, and I'd forgotten how much I missed hearing that. It wrapped me in comfort. "Okay, possibly the craziest thing you said in all of this is that you're completing your move after just a couple of days. Meanwhile, I still have a house full of stuff up here, and I am trying to just get more clothes down there so I'm not doing laundry every few days or buying new stuff."

"There are certain advantages to having no other responsibilities." I leaned in close to whisper, "Just a

235

reminder though, you're not exactly poor, so you could just hire it done."

His smile grew still larger. "Fair point. I'd like to find a permanent place though, so I can decide what comes down, what stays here. Make some sense of it rather than doing it randomly."

"I'd be happy to help you look, even help organize what you need to move."

I'd rooted myself in place, kind of afraid to move in case I broke the spell of the moment. Kyle, however, moved closer. The clean, citrus smell of his body wash filled my nose. I resisted leaning in or nuzzling his neck.

"I'm glad you're here." A vibration came down his arm, through his hand, and into me. "I promise to try not to be so intense going forward. All that's happened with us and the trade made it clear I need to talk more, jump to conclusions less, and, in general, be more flexible."

"Pressgrove, you've got about five minutes." Kyle turned and waved at a person I didn't know. So many new people to know in Phoenix.

"God, I'm sorry we can't go talk more."

I shook my head. "It's okay. I knew time would be short. I wanted to let you know what my plan was and that I want to give us the best possible shot."

The remaining gap between us closed as Kyle drew me into a tight hug—one I happily returned. After a moment with my head on his shoulder, he pulled back, and I looked at him. He grinned so big, and those beautiful eyes were so bright that I thought I could burst from happiness. He pressed his lips to mine, and I hungrily accepted the kiss, opening my mouth so our tongues meet.

"Damn it," Kyle said as his watch buzzed. "I'm sure

that's them telling me to get back over to the locker room so we can go."

He kissed me more, muffling the last part of that sentence. I enjoyed it for a moment before I gently dislodged myself from the hug.

"You should go. We'll see each other in just a few days."

He grinned again. "I can't wait. I'll call you tomorrow so we can talk more."

"I look forward to it."

"Me too," he said and hustled out the door.

He'd been gone mere seconds before he came charging back in. He kissed me hard and deep. I returned it with equal intensity. Every fiber of my being sparked for this man.

His breath came in short bursts when he pulled back. "Now I really do have to go. But I needed that to hold me over until I see you at home."

I nodded, left speechless. That kiss had overflowed with power, conviction—love.

I think we'd just marked our territory with each other.

My heart flew free. I hated having to let him go, but we'd have plenty of time at home. While we wouldn't live together, it said a lot that he'd just called Phoenix home.

## THIRTY-FIVE

### KYLE

FROM THE MOMENT a road trip began, I longed for it to end. It'd never been more true than for this one though.

And, yeah, Phoenix was home now. It hadn't clicked I'd said that to Austin until I was on the plane.

Austin and I talked every moment we could over the days I spent in New York and Nashville. He'd spent about half of those five days in Detroit before going to Phoenix. The place he'd bought was a couple of miles from the furnished rental I had.

My plan had been to deal with a proper house hunt in the off-season. But he'd offered to help me with that sooner. I'd certainly feel more settled if I had *my* place rather than something temporary.

As we landed at the airport, I looked out over the dark landscape. I still had a lot to get used to living here. Not just the warmer weather and no snow, but the overall energy was different than Detroit.

We were due to take the bus from the airport to the arena, where we'd all parked, and distribute luggage from there. Instead of dozing on the plane, I fidgeted, excited to see Austin tonight. We'd planned that I'd go to his place for a proper homecoming.

Once the fasten seatbelt sign was off, the team seemed like zombies meandering to get carry-ons and wander off the plane. I wanted to move faster.

As I made my way down the stairs, I had to do a double take. Austin waited planeside. He grinned widely.

What? How could he be here? It was so late even the fans who sometimes met the plane weren't here. He didn't even stand behind the fan barricades; he'd managed to be right here.

I sheepishly waved, which only broadened his smile.

The team didn't give him a second look. Word had traveled fast about us, even before I'd made it back to the locker room in Detroit. The team offered congratulations on our reconciliation before we'd left the arena. News got back to Phoenix fast too. By practice time in Nashville, Owen told me that the wives, girlfriends, and boyfriends stood ready to welcome the new guy into the fold. I hoped Austin was ready to have a lot of new friends. We'd run so hot and cold in Detroit, he hadn't gotten integrated into that group.

As I stepped onto the ground, I pivoted to my right instead of heading left with everybody else

He wrapped me in a hug. "Welcome home."

Home. A small part of me twinged at that—a bit of remorse from the kid who thought his allegiance should be elsewhere. I suspected that voice would always be there, but eventually it'd be softer.

Austin certainly felt like home. In his arms at the airport felt perfect.

We got some quiet awwws as he gave me a light kiss— nothing near as intense as that last one in Detroit had been.

That kiss was burned in my memory, and I'd recalled it often the past few days.

"I got permission to pick you up."

Wow.

I can't imagine the number of calls he'd had to make for that. Not to mention being allowed this close to the plane. My bag ended up next to us, and Lenny clapped me on the back and wished me good night. Austin had really set up a lot for this. No doubt there'd be some ribbing from the guys over the special attention—but I didn't care about that one bit.

"You need anything else?"

I shook my head. I had my bag and my backpack. My car could stay at the arena until tomorrow. "Let's go."

He took my hand and even took the roller bag. This played out like our very own romance novel.

"New car?" I dropped into the passenger seat of a Lexus after we stored my stuff in the trunk.

He settled in behind the steering wheel and started the car. "Rental. Just until mine gets here. It will be another couple of days before the truck arrives. I thought about going new, but I'd had mine so customized when I bought it that I didn't want to let it go."

I knew exactly what he meant. I'd be bringing my car down at some point as well.

My chest tingled—the perfect kind of tingle. It reminded me of the intense joy of scoring a game winner or seeing a kid I coached make his first successful slap shot or... being with the man I loved. There'd been moments like this before—the night in Vegas, the day we'd spent together, making late breakfast. I liked how much stronger it vibrated in me now.

"I got good news from my attorney tonight." Austin

sounded excited, which lately hadn't been the case when talking about legal things. "We signed the letter of understanding to transfer control of the foundation to me. It'll be fully mine, no longer connected to the company. It cost some money, but it was worth it."

I reached over and squeezed his leg as he drove. "That's great. Congrats." I left my hand where it was. I liked the connection. He'd desperately wanted the foundation and had to jump through some hoops to get it.

"My attorney's hopeful everything else wraps this week. I'm ready for the clean break."

"I'd never considered the idea of getting to reset everything." I yawned. "Sorry."

"You don't ever have to say sorry about being tired after a game and a flight." He dropped a hand from the steering wheel onto mine. "And I hadn't ever thought about starting over either. I'd gotten so much fear from my parents and ignored what could be. I don't want that Austin to ever show up again—if he does, send him to the penalty box."

"Duly noted. Hopefully, neither of us gets to that extreme. I'm sure we'll both fuck up. I have to be not so stubborn when it happens."

"Same here." He gripped my hand extra tight as I did the same to his leg.

We drifted into the most comfortable silence. That peace had been there with Austin from the start but had more impact now that we'd committed to each other.

He pulled into a neighborhood I'd been to one other time because Nick Belcroft, a D-man, lived here. He'd invited me for brunch along with Tristan Nettles. Nick, Tristan, and me made up the LGBTQ contingent on the team. Nick was married while Tristan had recently gone through a break up.

During our trip, Nick had extended an invitation for Austin and I to come over when we were situated.

The homes were new, nice, and weren't crazy big from what I'd seen. Nick had said he and his husband bought there because they knew another gay couple that lived in the neighborhood and spoke highly of its inclusiveness. Maybe I'd look here too.

Austin pulled up to a two-story, modern home and triggered the garage door. I couldn't make out all the details in the dark, but it seemed nice. The garage had space for his car, but more than a few boxes and other signs of a move-in in progress littered the other half.

We got out as the door closed behind us. I grabbed my backpack, and he got my luggage.

"Remember, this is all still a work-in-progress." He opened the door that led inside and lights turned on in the kitchen. The appliances were new—not ridiculously high-end but more like what Mom had installed when she'd renovated. Beyond that, it was a cozy kitchen that would be nice to hang out in for breakfast.

"I've got makings for Greta's pancakes," he said as if he'd read my mind. "I thought we could cook in the morning... if you'd be up for that. Seemed the perfect thing to break in the kitchen with."

"Great idea."

As we talked, soft lights came up. Had it come this way with the motion sensors or had he already had people here installing new stuff? I liked it. While the kitchen had turned on bright, the living room was softer.

"Let's go get comfortable," I nudged into him and gave a sleepy smile.

He nodded, and I followed him through the living room that only had a couple of chairs and a TV standing in front

JEFF ADAMS

of the fireplace. At the staircase by the front door, he said, "I'll give you the full tour in the morning, but down here is the kitchen, living room, bath, and a guest room. Upstairs is the master suite and my office."

We headed up.

"I like the layout even better seeing it for myself rather than the pictures."

"Me too. I like having all the personal space up here. There's a lot of custom stuff too—like those appliances and all the smart home stuff."

"I can't believe you got it so quick."

"Things happen fast when you deal in cash."

"Good to..." I stopped short as the lights came on in the master. He'd spent time with this. The king-sized bed dominated the room but didn't overtake it. It looked comfortable with many pillows at the headboard. He also had a loveseat and coffee table along with a dresser. Through one door, I saw a sliver of what looked like a spectacular shower and the other door had to be the closet.

"Like it?"

"Yes."

"I finished it first. Seemed like a good idea to have a good place to sleep."

He took my backpack, put it on the luggage, and parked them by the sofa.

I followed him. Once he'd let go of the luggage, I spun him around and kissed him. I couldn't hold back my hunger. With no one watching this time, I lost myself in him.

At least until I had to stop to yawn.

Damn it.

"Let's get some sleep," Austin said as he pushed the jacket off my shoulders. I helped get it off, and he laid it nicely on the seat behind him.

"But..."

"Uh-uh." He put a finger on my lips, and I had to grin. "We've got all day tomorrow, and we can do anything we want."

"Including staying naked in bed?" I unbuttoned my shirt as Austin pulled his light sweater over his head.

"Oh, hell yeah."

I couldn't decide where to put the shirt, and he took it from me. He opened the closet door and threw them both inside. Into a hamper, maybe?

"Can I talk you into maybe some fun now?" Damn it. My body really betrayed me with another yawn at the end of that. I toed off my loafers and then stripped off my slacks. I adjusted the hard-on in my boxer briefs as best I could.

Austin ditched the rest of his clothes, his arousal just as obvious as mine.

"This will wait." He gently grabbed my cock. "Come on."

As if we had a routine—although, it was the same pattern we'd done once before—we went to opposite sides of the bed, pulled back the covers, and situated some pillows. Wordlessly, we met in the middle of the bed, me on my back and Austin draped partially on me so we could kiss.

The bed was heavenly. He'd chosen well.

Austin next to me was so right. "I love you, Austin."

He crushed his lips into mine and sealed my declaration. "Love you too."

He laid his head on my shoulder and snuggled in before he called for the lights to turn off.

I looked forward to many more nights ending just like this.

# EPILOGUE
## KYLE

*NHL ALL-STAR WEEKEND, the following year*

Austin swallowed up my moans as he kissed me. My legs wrapped around him as he thrust deep inside me. No better way to wake up than with a horny Austin eager to work me over.

I cried out from bliss as he hit exactly the right spot.

"That's what I like to hear," he said as he broke the kiss.

Over the past few months, he'd discovered exactly how to work my prostate, and today he did an expert job pounding me hard and fast. Stars danced in front of my eyes, and every part of me was electrified.

"Fuck, fuck, fuck..." I tried for other words but couldn't form them. Austin had extra fire this morning. Locking my legs even tighter around him, I dropped my hands from his back to the bed so I could clench my fists around the sheets.

Hopefully this room had decent soundproofing or our neighbors were going to be very well aware that my boyfriend fucked my brains out.

"That's it," I finally managed to say. While Austin thrust, my cock occasionally brushed against his stomach as it bounced between us. The extra sensation pushed me ever closer to the edge. "You're going to make me lose it if you keep this up."

"Good."

I focused on him just long enough to see a sexy, evil glint in his eyes.

"You... know... I..." Getting words out as he drove into me wasn't easy. I took in a breath to try to get a whole sentence out. "I might not be able to skate tonight at this rate."

"Oh well—" He stopped, causing me to whimper. "I guess I better stop then." He pushed back against my legs, but I didn't let him slip out of me. No way he'd be able to break my hold.

"Fuck the skills competition." I used my feet to push against him, forcing him to go deeper.

"There you go." Austin resumed, finding another speed that caused me to slap the bed. "That's the right answer."

Somehow, he managed to increase the pleasure, and all I could do was go along for the blissful ride.

"Gonna come," I said in a mangled voice.

Between the insane things Austin was doing and the random touches my cock had against him, I didn't need anything else.

Suddenly, cum shot out as I clinched around Austin. I felt the warmth on my chin and chest as I came more than I thought reasonably possible since we'd also gotten off before we went to sleep only a few hours ago.

"Oh yeah, gonna do it too." Austin kept up the thrusts as he filled me up. His breath went ragged as he orgasmed. I was the loud one in this relationship while he had awesome cum-face—alternating between furrowed brow and the best open-eyed and open-mouthed look ever.

He gradually slowed and bent to deliver a passionate, loving kiss. He gently slipped out as his mouth stayed locked on mine. Our chests pressed together as he laid on me.

Shortly after he'd moved to Phoenix, we did the official testing to make sure we could do whatever we wanted condom-free. One of the best choices we'd made was to get that done before our first fuck. It made that night all the more special.

"I never get tired of owning your ass," Austin said as he gently rolled off me and onto the bed.

"The feeling's mutual. I love giving you a good, hard, proper fucking." I winked at him. "Of course, I also love you doing me."

"Such language. And on our anniversary."

We laughed. Our sex talk wasn't imaginative, but it did crack us up.

"Happy Anniversary!" I rolled toward him, bumping my sticky chest into his side. "I love you."

"I love you too."

We kissed for a while—a long while.

"I hope everyone is having as much fun as we are this morning." I rolled off the bed and opened the curtains so bright winter sunlight could flood in. While we were high up, I kept the sheers closed to not only maintain some privacy but to filter the light a bit.

We were in the hotel headquarters of game weekend, and it was a utilitarian hotel room with a king bed. We'd thought about popping for something extra to celebrate, but we'd decided to stay on the same floor with some of the other players.

"I doubt anyone got their boyfriend off as well as I did this morning."

I adored Austin's confidence. He'd gone from questioning his abilities in the bedroom because he'd had little experience before we got together to becoming an expert in no time.

"We need to get moving or we're going to be late." Austin padded from the bed to the coffee maker parked in the alcove between the main room and bathroom.

We were having a late breakfast with G, Layne, Slater and Ash. Not only did G and I end up with incredible guys, but those guys had too. Talk about an event bringing people together. It was a great group to be part of.

Tomorrow, NBCSN planned to interview the five of us about it to air as part of their weekend coverage.

Once Austin had a cup of coffee going, he came back and grabbed his phone from the nightstand. "Mom texted. They've all boarded, so they're on time to arrive here this afternoon."

The true revelation for the weekend was Austin's parents traveling with my mom for the game. Austin introduced me to them when we went to Detroit right as the off-season began. They were pleasant and reserved but did truly seem happy their son had someone.

Mom, however, got them out of their shell.

She'd insisted on meeting them but getting them to a restaurant was deemed a waste of money. So, she'd invited Harry and Justine over, wowed them with her lasagna, and by the end of the night, they'd gotten along as if they'd been friends for years.

Austin wasn't exactly sure how it had happened, but his parents indulged themselves periodically now—eating out, traveling a bit, and enjoying life more. Mom hasn't told either of us how she'd convinced them to do that, but I loved how Austin lit up anytime his parents told us about some adventure they'd taken.

"I've also got confirmation of my meeting this afternoon. It's during your fan zone time, so I won't miss much of our day."

"That's great." I crossed to him and nestled up to his side, resting my chin on his shoulder. "Are you feeling good about the presentation? You haven't talked much about it the past couple of days."

He put the phone down and pivoted so we were face-to-face in a loose hug. "All good. I feel great about what I've put together regarding what I can bring to them to enhance their interface designs."

"You're going to wow them." I kissed him on the nose.

"And if I don't, bringing them as VIPs to an All Star Game should help." He smiled and placed a kiss on my nose. This had become a thing for us.

"Nothing better than some hockey to help seal deals." I took his hand and led him to the bathroom. "Come on, we should get showered and grab some breakfast."

"I'd rather spend the day naked with you. I'm quite enjoying all this hanging out without clothes."

"I guarantee we'll end the day much like we started it."

He hummed an appreciative noise as I turned on the water to get it hot, and he got towels ready for when we were done.

One of the highlights of the past year was Austin winning me. Those first couple months were a roller coaster, but I wouldn't trade the rest of the year for anything because it set up an excellent future.

THANKS FOR READING *KEEPING KYLE!* Reviews are an incredibly valuable to spreading the word about great books. Please consider leaving a review about *Keeping Kyle* on your favorite retailer or review site.

**Want more?** Remember in Chapter 16 where Austin said he'd always wanted to go to someplace like Provincetown?

They do just that in *Kyle & Austin's Provincetown Vacation*. Go to JeffAndWill.com/Kyle-Extra, leave your email address and I'll send you the free short story.

# ACKNOWLEDGMENTS

Susan, thanks so much for coming up with the idea for a shared bachelor auction universe. And, RJ and V.L., thanks for thinking of me and for the invite come play along. I had a wonderful time creating Hockey Allies Bachelor Bid universe world alongside Chantal and the three of you. Extra thanks to RJ for allowing Garrett to be Kyle's best friend. I had a great time brainstorming with her about their long friendship.

Meredith, thank you for the stunning cover.

Kiki, I'm so glad I found you to be my editor. I loved working with you on this book and look forward to doing it again soon.

Jen Walter participated in a Facebook takeover I did in the MM Hockey Romance group, and she suggested the name Arsenal for Kyle's team. There were many great names thrown out, but Arsenal was *the* one. Thanks, Jen! (And, hey, if you're reading this and you're not in the MM Hockey Romance group, come join us!)

I wrote this book while I was a student in Rachael Herron's 90 Days to Done online course. I learned some great stuff during those twelve weeks to hone my craft. Thanks to Rachael and my classmates for being amazing. I loved working alongside you all as you wrote your own books (which I can't wait to read). They, along with my husband Will, helped me figure out some key events in the fourth act of *Keeping Kyle,* and I'm grateful to them!

Most importantly, thank you for reading. I hope you enjoyed Kyle and Austin's story!

## ALSO BY JEFF ADAMS

**Hockey Romance**

*Head in the Game*

*The Hockey Player's Heart (co-written with Will Knauss)*

*The Hockey Player's Snow Day*

*Keeping Kyle (A Hockey Allies Bachelor Bid Romance)*

*Rivals*

**On Stage Series**

*Dancing for Him*

*Love's Opening Night*

**More Romance Titles**

*A Sound Beginning*

*Room Service*

*Somewhere on Mackinac*

*Summer Heat*

---

**Young Adult Titles**

Each of these are available in ebook, paperback and audiobook

## ABOUT THE AUTHOR

Jeff Adams has written stories since he was in middle school and became a published author in 2009 when his first short stories were published. He writes both gay romance and LGBTQ young adult fiction...and there's usually a hockey player at the center of the story.

Jeff lives in central California with his husband of more than twenty years, Will. Some of his favorite things include the musicals *Rent* and *[title of show]*, the Detroit Red Wings and Pittsburgh Penguins hockey teams, and the reality TV competition *So You Think You Can Dance*. He, of course, loves to read, but there isn't enough space to list out his favorite books.

Jeff and Will are also podcasters. The *Big Gay Fiction Podcast* is a weekly show devoted to gay romance as well as pop culture. New episodes come out every Monday at BigGayFictionPodcast.com.

Learn more about Jeff, his books and find his social media links at JeffAdamsWrites.com. From the website you can also sign up for his newsletter to get a free ebook of *The Hockey Player's Snow Day*, as well serialized stories, previews of new books, book recommendations and more!

Made in the USA
Las Vegas, NV
13 April 2024

88666032R00148